A Hanging Offence

Don Cummer

Scholastic Canada Ltd.
Toronto New York London Auckland Sydney
Mexico City New Delhi Hong Kong Buenos Aires

Scholastic Canada Ltd.
604 King Street West, Toronto, Ontario M5V 1E1, Canada

Scholastic Inc.
557 Broadway, New York, NY 10012, USA

Scholastic Australia Pty Limited
PO Box 579, Gosford, NSW 2250, Australia

Scholastic New Zealand Limited
Private Bag 94407, Botany, Manukau 2163, New Zealand

Scholastic Children's Books
Euston House, 24 Eversholt Street, London NW1 1DB, UK

www.scholastic.ca

Library and Archives Canada Cataloguing in Publication

Cummer, Don, 1952-, author
A hanging offence / Don Cummer.

Sequel to: Brothers at war.
ISBN 978-1-4431-3908-3 (pbk.)

1. Canada--History--War of 1812--Juvenile fiction.
I. Title. II. Title: Brothers at war.

PS8605.U44H36 2015 jC813'.6 C2014-902440-1

Cover images: scene © J.T. Lewis/Shutterstock 1719501 RF; gallows © Natalia Bratslavsky/Fotolia 2619553 RF; soldier in silhouette © 2004 Silvia Pecota.

6 5 4 3 2 1 Printed in Canada 121 15 16 17 18 19

Table of Contents

For Jacob Cummer,
who explores with me the evolving relationships
between fathers and sons.

Queenston

October 1812

Hooves splash toward us and I step off the road. Father glances at me to make sure I'm safe, then squints into the telescope. His conversation doesn't skip a beat. "How many do you figure are beyond the trees over there?"

"Hard to tell," Mr. Secord replies. "Thousands?"

"Any artillery?"

"Up those cliffs, I'd think."

Father shifts the telescope and scans the cliffs on the other side of the river. Another rider gallops from the other direction. He splatters mud on our best Sunday clothes. Maybe we'll have to go back home now to change. Father steadies the telescope and scans the far shoreline. "Have you seen any boats?"

"I thought I saw some hidden downstream." Mr. Secord gently guides the position of the telescope. "Try over there."

Father grunts in agreement. He snaps the telescope closed and passes it back to Mr. Secord. He rubs his chin and contemplates the far shore. It's swarming with bluecoats. I've never seen so many soldiers. Too far away for a musket shot, but well within cannon range. We don't have many redcoats on this side, but we're scrambling to action. A squad of a dozen marches past double-quick up the road to the Heights.

"What can you see from up top?" asks Father. He nods up the cliffs to our right.

"There's a redan about halfway up," says his friend. "Want to look from there?"

Mr. Secord starts to lead us up the path, then stops and turns to me. "You'll have to stay here, young man."

"But — "

"Can't have children running around."

Who's he calling a child? General Brock himself sent me on a secret mission last summer. I look to Father for support. He gives me an apologetic smile. We must defer to our host.

"Go down to the house," says his friend. "You'll find the children there." The two of them climb up the slope to where the cannon points across the river.

* * *

"Eighteen . . . Nineteen . . . Twenty." Then I call out, "Ready or not, you're going to get caught." But I don't search among the gardens and houses. I head down to the dock. The children could be hiding there, couldn't they? I scan the far shoreline. Father and Mr. Secord are looking for cannons and boats — any signs that this is the place where the enemy plans to attack.

"Jacob . . . " a small voice calls from beneath the planks. Another voice giggles. To my right, the river rushes out from the cliffs. Upstream, it plunges over Niagara Falls. If I listen carefully I think I can hear a deep rumble. "Jacob," the voice whines, "you're not playing."

From this dock, longshoremen load supplies onto wagons to be hauled up the road past the Falls. On the other side of the river, another road leads up from *their* dock and men push at a wagon that is stuck in the mud.

"Jacob!" A girl's head pokes out from beneath the planks. "If you're not going to try to find us," Harriet scolds, "then maybe *you* should hide."

"Yes, Jacob," adds Charles. "You hide."

"Look! What's going on over there? They're trying to move that wagon." I try to interest them, but little Charles keeps tugging at my coat sleeve.

Harriet says, "You two hide and I'll count. One . . . Two . . . Three . . . "

"Look! Now there's a fight!" It's like watching an anthill from a great height, but even from across the water I can see two men punching at each other.

They've stripped off their blue coats and are swinging wildly.

"Four . . . Five . . . "

"Come on." Little Charles takes my hand. "I show you where hide."

And as if someone has kicked the anthill, men hurry down the road and swarm around the fight. Now an officer in a bicorne hat runs toward them. He's trying to push his way through the crowd and . . .

Someone has pushed the officer back! The officer raises his hand and . . . I can't believe it! Someone has just punched an *officer*. On our side of the river, he'd be stood against a wall and shot for that. Or at least flogged until he wished he were dead.

The fight has turned into a brawl. Everyone swinging at everyone. No, not quite everyone. One fellow backs toward their wharf. He turns and shakes his head and walks away. Even from this distance, he moves like Eli — that easy, lanky, loose-limbed stroll, as if nothing could bother him. A mop of black hair. Too far away to tell, really. But what if it's him — my blood brother, Eli McCabe?

"You gonna write to me?"

"Of course. You?"

"Yeah. Reckon."

That was four months ago, when Eli's family had to leave and go back across the river. Eli never was one for writing, but maybe he never got my letters either — not after the war began.

"Nineteen . . . Twenty! Ready or not, you're gonna get caught."

I wave to the figure on the far side of the river, but he's not looking this way.

"Jacob! Papa told you to play with us."

I give our secret call: a loon cry followed by three hoots of an owl. But the figure doesn't respond. That doesn't necessarily mean it's not Eli. Maybe he's too far away and can't hear me over the noise of the brawl. But whoever he is, he stands on the wharf, apart from it all, looking on. That's probably what I'd do too. Someone actually struck an *officer*!

"Eli!" I call out. "Eli McCabe!" Can a voice carry better than a loon call?

Bang!

A new sound in the distance — a pistol shot. The brawl stops. A man on horseback rides down the road. The smoke drifts away from where he holds a pistol in the air.

"Eli!" I call again.

But the boy on the wharf watches the horseman ride down their road, a horseman wearing a cocked hat with feathers. No ordinary officer. The soldiers begin to move up the road. I look back to the wharf. The solitary figure is gone, disappeared into the crowd.

"What's wrong, Jacob?" Charles looks up at me.

Harriet adds, "You feeling poorly? You want to sit down? You look like you've seen a ghost."

* * *

"Father?"

"Yes, Jacob."

"Is there going to be a battle?"

"It certainly looks like it."

The wagon rolls as our horse, Solomon, pulls us along under a canopy of yellow leaves. The sun is high in the sky but rain clouds gather again.

"Did you see cannons from up there on the redan? Boats?"

He shakes his head. "Just soldiers."

"How will they cross the river?"

"They would have boats hidden somewhere."

A raven soars ahead of us, lands in the trees and watches me.

"Did you see the fight?"

He shifts in the seat. "Very strange," he says.

"They'd never get away with that," I say. "Not in our army."

"Indeed."

"I think I saw Eli." Father looks at me. "I couldn't tell for sure. It was too far away." Solomon's footsteps suck through the muck. I pull my coat closer. The temperature is dropping ahead of the storm.

"Do you think he might be with the army?"

"He's not old enough," Father says. "And neither, young man, are you."

"So . . . if there's going to be a battle . . . "

He waits a moment for me to finish, but finally he says, "Yes?"

"Well . . . then . . . Shouldn't we turn around and go back home now? The militia will be expecting you."

He looks at me and laughs. "Have you been praying for a miracle?"

"Well, it's just that — "

"No, son. We'll stay in St. Davids tonight as we planned."

I fall into silence. I'd rather face the enemy army than what waits for me up the road. And the first drop of rain splatters on Father's top hat.

St. Davids

October 1812

I will never call her *mother.* Mrs. Lovelace is nothing like my mother.

Father sits stiffly in his cutaway coat and mud-splattered breeches, and I can tell by the way he holds his saucer he's nervous. But *she's* not nervous. This is her village and her house; her parlour, her furniture and her fine silverware. That's the portrait of *her* mother, and they look alike, their blond hair piled high, and the way they sit so straight. Her spine never touches the back of the chair. Her younger daughter pours tea. Her name is Georgina but they call her George. She probably thinks Fort George was named after her. Already she's taking possession of Father.

"Do you sell dresses, Papa? Fabric? That's wonderful. I'm sure Mama and I can make something very nice. And maybe jackets for you and young Jacob."

Young Jacob! Who's she calling young?

The older daughter — the brown-haired one — fidgets in her chair. When our eyes meet, she looks away. Her name is Abigail and they call her Abby.

"Is your pa gonna remarry?" Eli asked me after Mother died.

"Never. He loved Mother too much to marry anyone else."

"He's gotta have a wife, Jake. Otherwise he'll get ornery and a bit cuckoo. Women's a civilating influence."

A slight cough over by the sofa. Abby covers her mouth and her eyes meet mine. She nods slightly toward the door and I nod back. An ally in this house? Yes! Please! Get me out of here!

"Mama, would you excuse Jacob and me? I'd like to show him the village."

"In this rain?"

"I think it's stopped."

"You don't mind, do you, Mr. Gibson? Georgina, would you like to go too?"

"I'd rather stay here and talk to you and Papa."

Once outside, I push ahead of Abby.

"Where do you think you're going?" she calls.

"Don't care." I want to go home. Just follow the stream that tumbles down the Heights. Ten miles cross country, maybe, and the water will lead me back to Newark. But what would Father say? I can't leave him here.

"Want to see some salamanders?" she asks.

I stop and watch her head up the hill. Well, at least

salamanders are more interesting than tea parties.

Abby obviously thinks so too. Oblivious to the puddles, she splashes past the general store, a grist mill and the tavern where Father and I will sleep tonight. She cuts into the woods and climbs onto a log that has fallen over the stream, then stops and turns. "I can't believe she's calling your father *papa*. The dirt's still fresh on Papa's grave."

"I'm sorry."

"It's not your fault, Jacob. It's *her* way."

"No, I mean, I'm sorry about your father."

She surveys me. "It's because of the war, they say."

"Your father's death? I thought he was sick . . . "

"No. Mama getting remarried so soon." She begins crossing the log. "They say it's not safe any more. That she needs a man to help raise and protect us. That's what they say." She hops off on the other side and waits for me. "*I* say they should leave us alone!"

Crossing is harder than it looks. I hold out both hands for balance. When I've reached the other side, I say, "Everything's different now. Because of the war." I could tell her about all the bluecoats we saw this morning, but all I say is, "Something's going to happen soon." I jump down beside her. "I'm going to fight with the militia." That doesn't seem to impress her. "Maybe the flank company." She doesn't respond. "Maybe even with the regular army."

"You're too young."

"I'm almost old enough."

She tilts her head to look at me. "You're not sixteen. Nowhere near."

I pull myself to my full height, but it doesn't help much beside her. "Father was a hero in the last war and he wasn't much older than me."

She crinkles her nose. "I just wish they'd get it over with. Get things back to normal." Her eyes fill with tears and she looks away so I can't see. "Normal's dead." She brushes her eyes with the back of her hand, then kneels down to where a rotting log lies half-buried in the fallen leaves. She rolls it aside, and the salamanders lie there, sluggish in the cold. She gently pokes one and it creeps forward. I want to touch it too — pick it up and let it draw strength from the warmth of my palm — but I gesture to Abby to leave it alone and we squat on our heels and watch.

Abby looks at me and her eyes are dry again. "The old legends say that salamanders don't burn in a fire. Do you think that's true?"

"That's a phoenix," I reply.

"No, a phoenix burns, but it rises again. From the ashes."

I stare down at the salamanders, small and slippery, with their legs coming out at right angles.

Abby replaces the log, carefully and gently, then looks at me closely. "Your mother died *last* year, didn't she?" she says. "Is she still with you?"

"*What?*"

"Your mother."

I retort, "I still miss her, if that's what you mean."

She rises to her feet and I follow her. "Of course. But does she still stay with you?" Now she stops again and looks at me. "It's hard to explain, but it's as if Papa goes for walks with me. Out here. I feel close to him here." She crosses the stream back toward the village. "He's not here right now, but sometimes. Often. When I really need his comfort."

I follow her in silence. She's not the only one who feels that the dead are still with us. What if she's right? Are we being watched right now — by Mr. Lovelace, or even by Mother?

What I know for sure is this: Mother lay in the box in the candlelight, and when they carried it outside, it was our friends and neighbours who walked with us. That's what I know. I felt nothing — no sense of spirits accompanying us to the burying grounds. That's what I remember — what I hold onto when the night falls.

* * *

Father's breathing slows and deepens, but I stare up at the ceiling and listen. A branch taps against the glass in the wind. At least, I hope it's a branch. What if it's Mr. Lovelace watching from the window, wanting to come in? No, it's real wind, real branches, real rain — all from this world. And I have problems enough in this real world.

"Father?"

"Yes, Jacob," he mumbles.

"Where are they going to sleep?"

"What?"

"The Lovelace girls — where are they going to sleep?"

"You'll have to give up your room." The ropes beneath the mattress creak as he shifts. "Until we build the new house."

"I don't want a new house."

Father sighs. "You'll like it. It will be bigger."

"I like our old house." The rain splatters the glass. "Will *she* sleep in your room?"

"Who's *she*?" He's wide awake now.

"Mrs. Lovelace, then."

"She'll be Mrs. Gibson. You can call her *Mother*, you know." I hold my tongue. "You'll sleep on the trundle bed in the kitchen."

I'll be able to sleep with my dog, Ginger. Maybe there are some advantages to this after all.

"We'll build a new house in the spring." His voice grows sleepy again. "You'll have a room of your own."

My eyes grow heavy. I won't be able to stay awake much longer. "Will Ginger be able to stay in my room? The new one, I mean."

"Jacob, we're going to have to do a lot of things differently, but not that."

If Ginger could sleep beside me, then nothing would ever harm me — not even in my dreams.

I'm in the forest again. Dusk. I cannot see through the trees. A wolf barks. But it's not a wolf. It's a dog. It's Ginger and she will keep me safe. She is barking at me. Barking and barking. The way she does when something is wrong. But she is moving so slowly. As if we're floating in the lake and the water pushes against us. She barks slowly, and the sound is not her usual yapping, but low, rolling thunder.

I sit up in bed. "Father?"

He groans and rolls over. "Yes, Jacob," he murmurs.

"What's that sound?"

He bolts upright.

There it is again. Not thunder. Sharper, but just as deep.

"Guns!" he says. "Get dressed! It's begun."

* * *

Off to the east, the sky above the trees flashes. The dogs in every house and farm howl and bark in reply to the distant booming. We follow the tavern keeper's lantern through the mud to the stable, and I pull on my coat and stuff the tails of my nightshirt into my trousers. We harness Solomon to the wagon, and he huffs in discomfort as we lead him out into the rain. A man stumbles up the road, a musket in one hand, the other hand clamping down a floppy hat. Another man holds a lantern as he bullies the local militia into order. If we were back home, Father would be marshalling our neighbours.

"I'm coming with you."

"Out of the question."

"You were my age when — "

"End of discussion." He turns to me. "I need you to stay here to protect Mrs. Lovelace and the girls."

"But — "

"You have to promise me that you will help them. Well?"

I stare down at the mud. "Yes, sir."

* * *

The Lovelace women stand at their door, clutching their dressing gowns against the wind. Father climbs down from the wagon and I hop into the mud beside him.

"Can Jacob stay with you?"

"Of course. Will you go back to Newark?"

He shakes his head. "Straight to Queenston, I think."

She nods. "Take something to eat."

Their backs disappear into the kitchen. Georgina bounces behind them, but Abby stays with me in the lobby.

"You've got to help me," I whisper.

"Do what?"

I tell her my plan.

"That'll never work."

"It will if you help."

She pauses, then scurries upstairs. While the voices talk in the kitchen, she scampers back down carrying two woollen shirts. She thrusts one at me.

"Papa's," she tells me. I hide it under my coat.

The others return. I hate goodbyes. No one wants to say what's on everyone's mind: Father may not return. He reaches for Mrs. Lovelace's hand and lifts her fingers to his lips. His hair is dishevelled, and whiskers stubble his cheeks, but Mrs. Lovelace curtsies as if he were her prince. He pats Abby's shoulder. Georgina lunges forward to wrap her arms around his waist and press her face against his chest. She's sobbing. When he comes to me, he stoops with his hands on his knees so that our heads are at the same level.

"You protect Mrs. Lovelace and the girls," he says. When I don't reply, he adds, "I'll be back as soon as I can." Still I say nothing. He swallows and I hope I'm not going to cry. "You're growing into a fine young man, son. I love you, and I'm proud of you." He hugs me the way he used to when I was little, then rises and opens the door. We watch him climb into the wagon and pull his hat down and his collar up. I nudge Abby. *Now!*

"Mr. Gibson! Wait!"

She rushes out with a woollen shirt.

"Abby!" her mother scolds. "You'll catch your death!"

I make my move, with a quick glance back to Georgina. Her eyes are wide as cannon barrels. I put my finger to my lips.

Abby keeps Father's attention. "You'll need to stay warm." She climbs onto the wagon step to hand Father the shirt. When the box leans under her weight, I counterbalance with mine on the other side. It works! I slip behind the driver's seat unnoticed. Father snaps the reins and the wagon lurches forward.

Then Mrs. Lovelace detects the plan. "Jacob! Jacob! Mr. Gibson, wait!" Her voice recedes in the distance, drowned by the howling wind, the clamour of dogs and Solomon's hooves splashing.

Father is not listening to any of this. He's following the sound of the guns.

Into the Battle

October 1812

I curl up beneath the seat and hug the woollen shirt to my chest. This is not how I imagined going into battle. When Eli and I played, the sun always shone.

"I'm General Wolfe. We'll climb the cliffs and take the city."

"You just point the way, Gen'rul. I'll be at 'em."

"Charge!"

"Charge!"

In our battles, flags snapped, bugles blared, bayonets gleamed, and forward, forward, forward we attacked, heads high and our muskets blazing.

Musket. Uh-oh. Beside me on the floorboards, Father's musket and cartridge box lie wrapped in oilcloth. If I don't move them, he's going to find me when he retrieves them. With every pitch and jostle, I prod the package toward his feet. I can see his shoes now; morning is coming. The wind blusters and it carries the rotten-egg stench of gunpowder. The boom of guns grows louder. So does the *rat-a-tat-tat* of drums. The ragged crackle of a musket volley vibrates the wagon. I know that sound — have heard it often at home, drifting in the air from the parade ground in Fort George. But this volley is followed by a new sound. I've watched neighbours slaughter their pigs in the fall, and heard how they squeal in fear and agony. This is much worse. This is as if pigs could cry for their mothers — the sound men make when they're cut down by lead.

"Halt! You there!"

We roll to a stop. Another roar of musket fire. More howls of pain and rage.

"Gibson," Father calls. "Lincoln County militia, reporting for duty, sir."

"Gibson!" shouts a gruff Irish voice and it lowers as it gets closer. "Sure, you were here yesterday with Secord."

"Yes, Lieutenant."

"Let me show you the lay of the land." The springs creak as Father steps down. "The enemy's after crossing the river and they've landed below the cliffs. We're trying to push them back, but they're holding their own. Understood? Now, there are a few of your Lincolns below the town, if you want to join them, but right now, by the saints, we need you more up there."

"The redan?"

"Exactly."

"Then I'll climb the slope here and go around the fighting."

"That's grand. You'll not be needing your wagon, then. Sergeant McIlroy!"

"Sir!"

"Mr. Gibson has kindly brought us his rig. Carry on."

I curl up as small as I can as Father reaches under the seat and the musket drags heavily across the boards. A moment later, the oilcloth is tossed back. I raise my head cautiously. Father lopes toward the dark Heights. He's wearing his courting clothes and his buckled shoes. I have a moment when I can follow him, then the smoke swallows him up. Now what do I do? First thing: pull on this woollen shirt.

The wagon sags, followed by a painful groan.

"Jaysus, Kelly, you'll kill the poor bastard before we even get started. Jonesy, get up there and give us a hand."

At the back of the wagon, a redcoat soldier with a bandaged head hauls himself up and grabs the end of a blanket. A sergeant leaps up to help drag the blanket into the wagon. It carries an unconscious man.

The sergeant sees me. "What are *you* doing there?"

"I . . . I've come to help . . . sir?"

"Don't *sir* me. You drive this thing?"

"Y-yes, sir. I mean, yes, Sergeant."

"Good. Jonesy, you get up there and show him the way."

They load the wounded. The man with the bandaged head collapses on the seat beside me and nods wearily down the road. I snap the reins and Solomon pulls us forward into the village.

"Where are we going?"

The bandaged man nods forward and grunts, "Big house."

Solomon pulls at a brisk walk. We pass by the Secord house. No lights inside. Are they all hiding in the root cellar? *Ready or not, you're going to get caught* . . . Then Solomon stops and prances nervously. I flick the reins and he takes a tentative step, then another, then lurches forward and we all slam backward. The wounded in the wagon groan. On the side of the road lies a dead horse. It has no head — but the cabbages and pumpkins in the garden are covered with blood and pulp. A cannonball can do that to a horse. What can it do to a boy?

At the north end of the village, the big stone house is a dark shadow against the sky. A cannonball ricochets off the stone walls, sounding like the crack of winter ice on the lake. By a lantern in the doorway, a man with a bloody apron shouts to soldiers nearby. They gather around the wagon as I pull up.

A roar of gunfire — not back at the other end of the village, but right here at the edge of the bank, where the ground drops down to the river. Bugles. Drums. And now dozens rush forward. Where did all these soldiers come from?

A young lieutenant runs up. "You! Get this rig out of here!"

"Where?"

"Up the road. Out of range."

I snap the reins again and Solomon pulls across a bridge and the road climbs a ravine. We move against the flow of soldiers in red coats and militia in their dark civilian jackets. At the top, the farmland stretches north. Solomon will be safe here. I climb down and pull him forward to a rail fence.

Something moves in the field — coming toward me from the village in the dusk. Eyes shine in the grass and behind them, a bushy tail rises. A red fox trots through the field. From her mouth hangs the limp carcass of a rooster. She sees me and hesitates with one paw in the air. Then she looks ahead, trots by me. I follow across the road to the riverbank.

Below, the water swirls. To the east, the sky turns grey and the river rushes toward me from the blackness of the cliffs. A pall of mist drifts across the water, and from it emerges a dark shadow the size of a monster. It rotates in the eddies. Horns stick out toward the sky like the antennae of a giant bug. A bateau

— one of the big rowboats they use to carry freight. Two oars thrust up at wild angles, and another drags in the current. The boat breaks free of an eddy and drifts toward me.

Other shapes sprawl across the boat, some lying over the gunwales, some twisted on the benches, others curled like babies sleeping. They are men and, as the boat passes, one stares at me. For an instant, I think I should call out, but the boat continues to roll and turn in the river, and the man looks into space. He's dead. They're all dead, shot dead.

"What's the worst way to die?" asked Eli.

I thought a moment. "Hanging," I said. "If it doesn't break your neck, you strangle to death." And I made a choking sound as I throttled my neck with my hands.

He laughed. "Naw. It would be worse to be stabbed and see all your guts come out."

We considered that while we sucked on our grass tips.

"Best way?" I asked.

"Shot," he said.

"Shot," I agreed.

These men are as dead as if they'd been killed by any other method. The man who stares at me has only one eye — a hole where his other would be. The boat drifts north toward the darkness.

What's that sound? From the north, it rolls toward me like a slow wave until I recognize it as the cheers of hundreds of men. The sound grows closer and clearer, and now I hear another sound: hoof beats. I rush back to the road. A horseman canters toward me, and the huzzahs follow him like the wake of a canoe. I recognize him in an instant: such a big man on a big horse, General Brock in his cape and his cocked hat. The way to the village below is crowded with soldiers, but they part before him. I didn't know where I was going, but my duty now is clear: I will follow General Brock.

The General

October 1812

General Brock is the greatest man I've ever met — probably the greatest man that any of us will ever know. Eli and I used to watch him sitting on a big rock on the riverbank, staring out at Fort Niagara on the other side.

"What's he doing?"

"Shhh. He's thinking."

"What about?"

"I don't know, Eli. How to win if there's a war, I guess."

"Reckon that takes a lot of thinking."

Now he's come to lead us into battle and canters toward the village. I try to follow, but the road fills again with soldiers stumbling up the ravine. A man in a bloody jacket limps as his comrade supports his weight. He looks at me, then away. He carries no weapon: a prisoner — young, but not as young as the guard who hovers at the side of the road, his musket at the ready.

I know this guard! Even with his face black with gunpowder, he looks like a dandy with a perfectly tied silk cravat around his neck.

"William!" I call. "William Dunwoody!" In Newark, I used to cross the street to avoid him. Now I'm just happy to see a familiar face.

"Gibson!" He stops and looks down his nose at me. "What the devil are you doing here?" His eyes resume scanning the prisoners, and I turn around and keep pace beside him.

"I'm so glad to see you!"

He looks me up and down again. "Is that your nightshirt? You should be home in bed." It's true: the tail of my nightshirt has come loose from my trousers and flops below my coat and the woollen shirt. I stuff it back in, then trot to catch up.

"Were you in the battle?" I ask.

Over the past months, I haven't seen much of William or Henry. Now that Eli's gone, they leave me alone. Out here on the battlefield, an arch-enemy doesn't seem like such an enemy any more.

But he still seems arch. "Not much of a battle," he says without looking at me. "More like a turkey shoot."

"But you were there. Right?"

"I'm here, am I not? But what are *you* doing here?"

A voice calls, "Is that Jacob Gibson? Are we that hard up for soldiers?"

Henry Ecker hurries up the ravine, trailing his

musket. Even among these soldiers — these grown men — Henry looks big.

"General Brock has arrived to save the day," William says with a smirk. "And Gibson here has followed to clean up after his horse."

"You there!" a voice shouts from the other side of the road. A sergeant points at us. "No loitering with the locals."

"Yes, Sergeant."

William hurries to the front of the column of prisoners.

"It's not fair," mutters Henry. "We're flank companies. We're supposed to be fighting, not guarding prisoners."

"What was it like?" I ask him. "Down there in the ravine?"

He grins. "Best time of my life." But the smile fades. "Now we're on this prisoner detail. Hope the war isn't over. I want to do it again."

"You! Colonial boy!" the voice shouts at Henry. "Get on with your job. We're watching this lot. I don't want to waste my time watching you."

"Yes, Sergeant," Henry calls. The column of prisoners moves slowly past us. One man staggers toward the grass. Henry butts him with his musket to force him back onto the road.

"I'd just as soon bayonet these poor devils and get back into the action."

From the other side of the village, the crackle of musket fire makes the whole column stop and each man turns to watch.

"You!" shouts the sergeant. "Move along!"

But no one budges. Up beyond the village, in the darkness of the Heights, the shooting increases. In the morning light, gunpowder clouds rise from the trees. Men in red coats scramble down the hillside and flee for the village. One man wears a dark coat — Father!

A prisoner cheers, then they're all cheering. I don't take my eyes off that dark-coated figure. He has a hundred yards to reach the safety of the houses. Fifty yards. I lose sight of him past the rooftops. Blue soldiers swarm in pursuit.

"They've taken the high ground and the cannon," says Henry Ecker. "We're in trouble now."

"Move!" shouts the sergeant. "*Now!*"

Henry raises his musket and clicks back the flintlock. He jabs at the nearest prisoner.

"We should be back there," Henry mutters, "taking back the Heights!"

"You! Colonial!" shouts the sergeant. "Keep those prisoners in line, or I swear I'll shoot you myself."

Henry turns to follow the column, but he gives me one parting look. He envies me. Me! He must escort prisoners. I'm free to follow the guns.

* * *

I run through the village, and a strange sound whizzes past my ear, like the biggest, fastest, angriest hornet ever. Something smacks into the house behind me. More whizzing. *I'm under fire!* But what's happening to my guts? Not *now*! Oh please, not now! I have to find an outhouse somewhere, fast. No time; I can't hold it in. I step behind a tree and whip the suspenders off my shoulders and drop my trousers. I finish the job and rise to my feet. *Get yourself together, Jacob.* Up go the suspenders and I run forward again.

At the foot of the Heights, General Brock's red uniform and golden epaulettes stand out so bright. He steps onto the stones of a low wall, crosses over and turns to face the troops as he draws his sword and holds it horizontally — the signal to form a line. I've seen captains do this, but never a general. Yes, this is the real thing. This is glory. But where's Father? A few dark militia coats have joined the attack, but I don't see him.

General Brock waves his line forward, over the wall and up the hill. I need a weapon so I can join them.

A soldier topples over and squirms to take shelter behind the wall. Blood oozes through his trouser leg. He tears a strip off his shirt and wraps it tightly around his calf.

"Please, sir. Can I take your musket? Your cartridge box too?"

He looks up, his face contorted. "Hand me that bayonet," he says. I pick up his musket and twist the bayonet from the barrel and give it to him. He pokes the bayonet through the knot on the bandage and turns it tight. "How old are you?"

"Almost sixteen."

He scoffs, "And I'm the Duke of York." He shrugs and I slip the strap of his cartridge box onto my shoulder and scramble over the wall. In our mock battles, I could hurl sticks around like Hercules, but this musket is so heavy that if I swing it, I'll be spun around after it.

I catch up to our soldiers. A redcoat looks sideways at me and his eyes widen. "Go home, boy," he shouts. "Get back to your family." I ignore him and press on. At the head of our attack, General Brock waves his sword and urges us forward. Not far to go now. We'll sweep them right up to the edge of the cliffs.

And then . . . the unimaginable.

A blue soldier steps out from behind a tree, cool and calm as he squints down his musket barrel, and the smoke belches. The General topples over. I hesitate. Everyone freezes. Soldiers gather around our hero, but a cannonball smashes through them, and one man tumbles over the General's body, his shoulder ripped away. A sergeant shouts, "Up! *Up!* Avenge the General!"

Ahead, the smoke has cleared, but the blue soldier has disappeared into the line forming among the trees. Where did they all come from? I raise my musket and squeeze the trigger. The flintlock cracks, but there's no flash of powder.

Stand your ground! Reload! My fingers fumble with a cartridge and I bite the paper off, the way Father taught me. The taste of gunpowder makes me want to gag. I try to pour powder into the priming pan, but I can't steady my hands. I look up again. There are no red soldiers near — they've fled toward the village. The blue line advances through the trees, and I turn and run. I want to throw the musket away so I can run faster, but I hold on. A bullet tears through my coat as I leap the wall. Where can I go? How far to the Secord house?

Up through the village, an officer on horseback trots toward me, the mud flying. "Come on, lads!" he shouts. "One more time!"

I know this man. He was with General Brock the day the General came to our house. Lieutenant Colonel Macdonell will finish what General Brock began: retake the cannon. I squeeze between two soldiers near Macdonell and his horse. A sergeant orders us into line, and then we move slowly through the trees toward where the blue line waits.

"Halt!" shouts a captain off to my left.

"Halt!" repeats the sergeant behind me.

"Make ready!" I hold the musket before me at an angle. I feel like a real soldier now.

"Preee-sent!" shouts the sergeant.

I raise the Brown Bess, although I know it's not loaded.

"Fire!"

The noise rocks into my chest and we're engulfed in smoke. The flash of powder from the man firing beside me scorches my cheek.

"Reload."

My hands are steadier now, but I still have a tough time finding the muzzle with the tip of my ramrod.

"Advance!" bawls the sergeant. We move through our own smoke and I can see the blue lines ahead.

"Halt!" "Make ready!" "Preee-sent!" I raise my musket. Breathe! Exhale! Hold steady.

"Fire!"

I close my eyes and squeeze the trigger. The musket kicks back into my shoulder like someone has hit me with a club.

"Reload!" calls the sergeant. I tear the cartridge paper open and prime the pan. Down the barrel goes the powder, the bullet and paper. Reach for the ramrod.

Uh-oh . . .

Where's my ramrod? Did I forget to take it out of the barrel? I've shot it away!

"Advance steadily," the captain calls out. "Charge them home."

"Fix bayonets!" shouts the sergeant.

I don't have a bayonet — it's tightening the tourniquet on a soldier's leg. I don't have a ramrod — it's probably stuck in a tree out there like an Indian's arrow. I cannot swing the heavy musket without spinning myself off balance.

"Advance!"

The blue line is obscured by smoke and flame. Those angry hornets whiz by again. I don't dare look to the side. We march forward, and when the smoke drifts away in the wind, we're so close I can see the buttons on the blue uniforms.

"Charge!"

Ahead, the blue line is breaking. They're falling back. The soldier on my right smashes a blue soldier with the butt of his musket. We're pushing them back — we'll push them right to the cliffs.

But the Colonel's horse rears and I duck to avoid his hoof. A sharp cry, and Macdonell himself hurtles to the ground. He tries to rise to his feet, but his legs will not obey. He reaches out to an officer who runs to help, but spins wildly and collapses.

"Forward! Forward! Don't stop!" a captain yells, but his hat is knocked from his head, replaced with a mat of red as though he's been scalped. He goes down.

The enemy is coming. I throw away the Brown Bess and pick up another with a bayonet attached.

The soldier won't need it. He's lying face down. Our soldiers pick up Colonel Macdonell and carry him back toward the village. It seems only moments ago they did the same with General Brock. Who's in charge now? What do I do?

The blue soldiers rush toward us. I trip over the legs of the dead horse and the musket flies from my hands. The hard ground knocks the wind out of me and I gasp for breath and then just lie there, very still, my nose buried in the rotting leaves.

A big shoe pushes down the sodden earth beside my face. Another stumbles over my hip. Then they've passed me, and the shouts and the firing fade down the slope. I peer over the carcass of the horse. The fight has moved toward the village. Red soldiers flee beyond the houses. Blue soldiers kick down the doors and swoop inside.

I know what Eli would say. "*We been whupped, Slim. Whupped real bad.*"

Worse: we've lost General Brock. I'm covered with mud and wet leaves, and the soggy tails of my nightshirt hang to the ground. Some warrior! I must look like the village idiot who has lost his way.

And maybe that's not a bad thing.

I rise to my feet, unbutton a suspender and untuck the last bit of my nightshirt so it hangs down past my knees. I remove my coat and the shirt Abby gave me, roll them up and hold them across my chest with both arms. I'm cold and wet, but the sun is beginning to burn through the clouds and it will be warmer soon. I can do this.

I stumble my way back down the slope. Two blue soldiers bandage a wounded comrade, and all three look up at me and stare.

"Hey! Boy! Where you goin'?" says one.

Keep walking, eyes straight ahead.

"Looks like we done liberated the madhouse," says the other.

The wounded man grits his teeth and tries to joke. "President Madison says hello." He groans as they lift him to his feet.

Coming toward me, bluecoat soldiers prod a ragged band of redcoat prisoners. How long ago did I talk to William and Henry? One hour? Maybe two? They were the guards then and the bluecoats the prisoners. Now everything's upside down. Keep walking, left, right, left, right, eyes straight ahead. Who is going to pay attention to a boy in a nightshirt? Some prisoners wear the dark coats of the Lincoln County militia. I hope no one recognizes me.

Then I see him — Father, his head down as he shuffles beside the bluecoat talking to him. I want to run and throw my arms around him, but I keep stumbling forward as if half-asleep. Closer now, and still Father has not raised his eyes.

The others stare at me: the exhausted, shamed

prisoners, and their exhausted, smug captors. I'm just one of the weird things that happens in war — something to laugh about tonight around the campfires: the lunatic boy in his nightshirt, staggering down the hillside.

Father listens to the bluecoat and shakes his head. Then he looks up and I stare at the road to avoid his glance. A prisoner curses. I lift my eyes and Father stands frozen while others stumble into him. His mouth gapes as he stares at me.

The guard talking to him turns to see what the fuss is about. Our eyes meet.

I stop dead cold and so does the bluecoat. I know those blue eyes, that shock of black hair poking below his shako. I know that this veteran of the battle — this victor guarding my father — is not much older than me.

I'm looking into the eyes of my blood brother, Eli McCabe.

The Mohawk

October 1812

Keep moving. Father will be safe if I keep moving. Left. Right.

"Slim?" says Eli.

Don't look. Don't call attention to yourself. Or to Father. Might get Eli into trouble too.

"Slim!"

Left. Right. Left. Right. Everyone stares at me now. The prisoners trip over one another.

"Move! Move along!" shouts an officer.

A ruckus in the column. I risk one glance back. Father tries to push his way through. The officer lifts a pistol and takes aim at his head, and Father slowly raises his hands into the air. His eyes meet mine, then shift back to the pistol.

A bluecoat steps toward me. "Son? You all right?" I cling to the bundle of clothes. Left. Right. Am I saying this out loud? The bluecoat steps aside and no one stops me, not here and not at the battle line forming along the road. I fix my eyes on the trees in the distance. Left. Right. Blue soldiers stand aside. The sun breaks through the clouds, but the road leads into the cold shadows of the forest. Left, right, every step closer to safety, but away from Father and Eli.

Father has survived. He's alive. A prisoner. I wish he hadn't seen me. He'll be so worried now. What will the American soldiers do with him? Send him south?

And Eli! Still the same bright eyes.

He's with *them*.

When we first met, we were two skinny boys at a snowball fight, trying to impress the older ones. Eli was small, but he was strong enough to keep me from falling through the river ice until help arrived. Now he carries a musket and wears the victors' uniform. I'll bet he didn't shoot away *his* ramrod.

We need to talk — meet at the lighthouse, where we once pledged allegiance. Seems so long ago.

When the road takes me deeper into the forest, over a rise and around a bend, I dare to look back. The blue soldiers haven't followed. I tuck my night-shirt into my trousers and pull on the shirt and coat. Water drips from the branches high above me.

What now? I'm so hungry. Father took food with him. He knew what it would be like. I could ask a farmer for food, but now that we've lost, the farmers might side with the enemy.

A cannon booms in the distance. Someone's still fighting back there. Crows flap overhead toward the battlefield. I can hear them caw, beyond the ringing in my ears.

I hear the *slop, slop, slop* of my own shoes through mud, and a squirrel who nags from a branch. No sound of birds now — strangely silent. Left, right, left, right.

Then . . . Moccasined feet block my path.

I look up.

A face painted and hideous. Red and black. Feathers. Bear claws.

I shout so loud my soul will surely chase after my voice. A musket bars my way. Eyes glare white against black paint. A mouth is a hard red line. A warrior. I raise my hands in surrender. His eyes never leave mine, but he takes the musket in one hand and slips a tomahawk from his sash with the other. He looks past me and tosses the tomahawk. It rises in an arc above me, but I duck anyway and cover my head with my arms.

Someone laughs. I peek. More warriors with feathers in their scalp locks. I raise my head. To the left, three stand to the side of the road. Two more wait on the other side, where a deer path disappears into the woods. They cradle muskets in their arms and smile at some shared joke. The joke, it seems, is me.

Slowly I turn. A tall man has caught the tomahawk

and slips it into the sash around his waist. His face is painted red and black. The feathers on his head cascade to his shoulders.

"Master Jacob Gibson!" he says. "Didn't expect to find *you* here." His accent is Scottish. I search his eyes.

"Mr. *Norton*?"

His eyes flash annoyance. "Teyoninhokarawen," he corrects. "And where," he continues, "is your Father?"

I don't answer. I stare as other warriors emerge from the forest. Eight. Ten. They emerge into the dappled sun, look at me and gather around Mr. Norton. They point to me and talk to one another in Mohawk. Through the yellow and orange leaves, there is no one, then there is someone. Then several. Then many.

A chirp as bright as sparrow song.

"Tchay-cub!"

A boy sprints past the older warriors. He wears trousers in the autumn chill. The last I saw him, he wore only a breechcloth.

"Ronhnhí:io!" I use his Mohawk name and rush forward to throw my arms around Good Spirit.

But his hands push back. This is a serious time — a time for Mohawk names and manly comportment. He pulls himself as tall as he can, but he's smaller even than me. Among the warriors he strives to be fierce and proud. He lifts his chin as he takes my forearm with one hand, my bicep with the other. His arm is slippery with bear grease.

"You hungry?" He rubs his stomach.

"Yes!"

He pulls a strip of dried meat from a deerskin bag hanging from his shoulder. I chew eagerly. Dried meat never tasted so good. Good Spirit chews on his own piece of jerky while we watch more warriors file out of the forest.

The last warrior emerges from the trees and I recognize his bad eye — the colour of summer cloud — and the gash down the length of his face: Tako'skó:wa — the Mountain Lion. He still wears the powder horn Father once gave him. He takes my shoulders in his hands and smiles with his missing teeth. Then he takes my hand with both of his and presses it against his heart. I can feel it beat. He places his right hand on my heart, and his smile grows. He says something in Mohawk, and whether Mr. Norton is translating for him or repeating his own question, or both, I don't know.

"Where is your father?" Mr. Norton says again. "And where is Mr. Willcocks?"

He Has a Good Spirit

August 1812

When Father was a boy, he left the smoking ruins of his home in the Mohawk Valley and joined the refugees who fled to Canada. Many of his friends and neighbours among the Iroquois also escaped, moving fast through the forest trails, the rebels in pursuit. Father and the other whites built new homes on the shores of Lake Ontario. The Iroquois moved further west to the Grand River. That was the last war. Father never likes to talk about those days.

General Brock used Father's ties to the Iroquois when he sent him with his friend, Mr. Willcocks, on a mission to the Grand River this past summer. I got to go because Father wanted me to know some of the world beyond our community. I was looking forward to getting away from the routines of my own town.

British soldiers loaded a wagon with bales of blankets and cloth coats, kettles and dishes, lanterns and axes, all hidden beneath the canvas cover.

And firearms: Brown Bess muskets, rifled muskets and smaller muskets too — designed for forest warfare, Father said.

"Tell *no one* about this," Father warned. "Not where you are going. Not who sends us. And above all, not what's in the wagon. This is a secret mission — General Brock's orders."

Whom would I tell? Eli had already left for the United States. I hadn't even told him when General Brock came to visit us. We had been quarrelling.

Father and Mr. Willcocks took turns driving two big horses that pulled the wagon up the road to the head of the lake. At a crossroads, we turned and followed the setting sun. A few miles from Mohawk Village, we stopped at a tavern for the night.

Mr. Willcocks went to bed early. "Big day tomorrow, gentlemen." He flopped down without even removing his boots. "Bright-eyed and bushy-tailed. Right?" He looked neither bright-eyed nor bushy-tailed. His red hair was plastered with sweat. The next day, he was too sick to travel. "Deliver the gifts, Robert," he told Father. He grimaced with a cramp, and took a breath. "We'll parlay later." Another breath. "I'll be right as" — he buckled and hissed through his teeth — "roosters."

By noon the next day, the air was muggy, and in the trees, the heat bugs rattled. The horses' hooves beat a steady drum and raised little clouds of dust. I had been hoping for something different than the streets of Newark but, along the road, the Mohawk farms and houses looked like the buildings back home. Where they worked in the fields of corn and squash, women and children shielded their eyes against the sun and waved to us as we passed. Dogs ran out from the shadows, barked at the rolling wheels a few times, then returned to the shade.

Father passed me a canteen. "Do you remember the Lovelace family? Two girls, Abigail and Georgina?" I recalled them from the church socials. "Their father has died."

I remembered the father. He sat in a rocking chair in the shade with a blanket over his legs, even in the heat of the strawberry season. "That's sad."

"Reverend Addison has suggested I go out to visit the Widow Lovelace and the girls."

The road dropped, and I could see the river in the distance. We entered the shade and that was a relief.

"May I go too?"

"Perhaps next time."

Next time? Why would there be a *next* time?

My lips shaped the question. But, instead, I shouted, "Ow!" My cheek stung, and when I touched it, my fingers came away wet with rotten crabapple. High, shrill whoops shrieked from the trees. Father lurched forward to catch his hat as it toppled over, a big welt of crabapple juice along the crown.

"What's going on?"

"We've arrived," he replied, and he whipped the horses to a canter.

Shrieks rang out from either side of the road, and mixed with them . . . laughter? A summer storm of crabapples, acorns and berries rained down on us. A boy behind a bush stepped out to hurl something.

"Hey! Stop!"

But the child waved a stick and grinned. A smaller boy toddled behind, thumb in his mouth. I could see others now as they rose from behind the willows and pelted us.

Ahead, another boy stepped to the side of the road as we hurtled past. He wore only a breechcloth. He shouted something at the younger boys, and it sounded like a scolding.

As we passed, his eyes briefly looked up and met mine and he nodded hello. I leaned over and looked back down the road. The boy talked to the children, and they hung their heads ruefully.

We slowed the horses to a walk as we approached the river. Father pulled them to a stop to let them drink. I removed my shoes, climbed down and filled the canteen, savouring the chill of the water. That boy had the right idea, I thought: if all I wore was a breechcloth, I'd plunge into the coolness right now. I looked up, and the boy was standing on the riverbank behind me.

"You Willcocks?" he called up to Father.

Father replied in Mohawk and the boy smiled. He climbed up into my place — *my* place! "Grandfather wait for you," he said. "Teyoninhokarawen wait too. I take you."

I hauled myself up. "That's where *I* was sitting," I complained. The boy just smiled at me as if I'd said something agreeable about the weather. He moved over so I could sit beside him. I took a closer look at this interloper. He could have been my age — it was hard to tell. The boy asked Father something in Mohawk and glanced at me when Father replied. When the boy asked another question, Father said, "Jacob."

"Tchay-cub," the boy repeated. He turned to me and grinned and pointed to his own chest. "Loon-hee-yo," he said.

Father added, "Say, it, Jacob: Ronhnhí:io."

I stumbled, "*Loon . . . loon . . .* "

"Ronhnhí:io," repeated the boy.

"It translates as *He has a good spirit*," said Father. "It's a good name, don't you think?"

I didn't know what to think. This boy had taken my place beside Father. Then, without another word, he turned and climbed into the back of the wagon.

"Hey, you're not supposed to go there," I warned.

Good Spirit just grinned and picked his way over the bundles. He picked up a hat and tried it on.

"Put that down." I seized the hat and put it back with the others. He reached down for a lantern and opened and closed its door. I snatched it from him. "These things belong to General Brock."

"Jacob, pay attention here."

"But . . . "

"Come sit with me."

The horses humped up the other side of the river, and I could see a church spire in the distance. The village was smaller than Newark, but the homes and gardens would have fit right in our town. Everything seemed so normal, right down to the chickens pecking in the yards and the occasional pig walking across the road.

From the front steps of a house, three men stared at us and frowned.

"They're not happy to see us," I said.

"They probably don't like what we're trying to do," Father replied.

"Why not?"

"Some here don't want to join General Brock."

"But they have to help defend our country."

"Upper Canada is not their country. The King's fight is not their fight."

"But they have to join us. Don't they?"

"Our king is not even their king. And some think they should fight for the other side."

"But that's treason!"

Father shook his head. "We have to negotiate."

Why should I be surprised? Newark was no different: some people thought we would be better off as part of the United States.

We approached the church and another group of people who seemed happier to see us. Four women stood in the centre and at the front of the group. Among the men, I recognized one familiar face: the blind eye and jagged scar of Father's old friend, Mountain Lion.

Father reined the horses to a halt, and a tall man stepped forward.

"I'm Norton," he said. He stood with the poise of a king. "Here I am called Teyoninhokarawen. How do you do?" His accent was Scottish. Father stepped down from the wagon and offered his hand. The tall man bowed as he took it. "Is Mr. Willcocks not with you?" he asked and he took Father's elbow as he led him toward the others. "We did not know what time you would arrive, of course. But we've managed to assemble a small welcoming party."

"I've brought gifts," said Father.

"Indeed."

I looked back into the wagon but Good Spirit was gone. No, there he was, among the adults now, standing in his breechcloth and moccasins, right beside Mountain Lion.

"You and Tako'skó:wa are old friends, I am told,"

continued Mr. Norton. Mountain Lion gave that warm, fierce smile I sometimes see in my dreams — the scarred face, the broken nose. "And I believe," Mr. Norton added, "you've now met his grandson, Ronhnhí:io."

Mountain Lion's grandson was *this* boy? He seemed so different from his grandfather, a man of quiet dignity.

* * *

This is how I remember meeting the man Father calls Mountain Lion, that winter long ago. Father drives the sleigh and Solomon pulls us far down the forest road. We smell the smoke of a campfire. Father pulls the reins and the harness bells fall silent. A chickadee dees in the distance. Through the trees, a man hangs a deer carcass from a bough. "He's on our land," I whisper. "He can't do that here." I look at Father's eyes. "Can he?"

Father takes his musket and wades through the snow toward the camp. He raises his hand in greeting, and the trespasser does the same. When Father reaches the firm snow of the campsite, he calls to me to follow.

By the time I have followed Father's trail to the camp, they have pulled out their clay pipes. They speak in words I do not understand — the language Father learned as a boy in the Mohawk Valley.

Father introduces me and I cannot pronounce the stranger's name. Father has me repeat it many times. Tako'skó:wa. It means the Mountain Lion, and when he smiles, gaps show where the teeth are missing. His nose is crooked like someone has smashed it. A scar slashes his left cheek from the corner of a blind eye, clouded as milk in tea. He would look fierce but for his warm smile.

While they talk, I wander over to where the carcass hangs, the hide pulled down and the meat red and rippled with white. Do people look like this, with their skin stripped away and their guts removed? Dominie Burns says the English pulled out the guts of the Scottish rebel, William Wallace, before they chopped his head off, and Henry Ecker says that, back in the wars with the French, Indians used to do that to their prisoners. Henry should know. His father grew up in the Mohawk Valley, just like mine. Once I tried to ask Father whether what Henry said was true, and he looked at me so sadly that I never asked him again.

Mountain Lion joins me and carves steaks from the carcass and wraps them in hide for us. Father puts the package on the ground at his feet and lifts his scrimshawed powder horn and its strap from over his head. Mountain Lion admires the drawing, slips the strap over his shoulder and sits proud as a king.

Then he reaches to his sash and brings out a folded square of deerskin. He hands it across the fire and nods for me to take it. I glance at Father and then reach for it.

"Thank you," I say softly and I unwrap it carefully. It contains the claw of a large animal. I fold the leather up again and place it in my pocket. I can feel my knife there. I take it out and hand it to Tako'skó:wa. He nods and smiles.

* * *

Father and I sleigh back toward Newark that evening. I sit in silence. After it has gone long enough, I complain, "You gave away your powder horn."

"Yes."

"I liked that powder horn. It was beautiful. And you traded it for some *meat*?"

"Yes," he says. "I guess it belongs to me now."

"Pardon?"

"Nothing belongs to you until you can give it away."

"That doesn't make sense."

He chuckles, as if there's some private joke. "Your mother would agree. But that's how we've lived and that's how we've become rich."

"We're not rich. Not like Magistrate Dunwoody."

"Jacob, we're rich in friendship — and in our love for one another."

"Because we give things away?"

"Not exactly. But it's what we do."

"We'll eat the meat and it will be gone. I *liked* that powder horn. It was a bad trade."

He smiles at me. "But you've made a new friend today. And believe me, Tako'skó:wa will be a *good* friend."

I listen to the harness bells jingle in the dusk. "I guess that knife is mine now."

"That's right," he says and he wraps his arm around me and pulls me toward him and away from the cold.

When I get home, I show Mother what Mountain Lion has given me. She sews a thong onto the leather so I can wear it under my shirt. Eli has it now, my gift before he left for the United States.

War Dance

August 1812

The sun went down, but the air still hung heavy with heat. Rather than have us return to the tavern and Mr. Willcocks, Good Spirit's mother invited Father and me to sleep in their home. She was a very important woman in this community, and Father told me that the invitation was a great honour. She was kind and gracious, and welcomed us in a way that reminded me of how Mother used to greet our guests.

But as twilight faded and the night grew dark, I was not so sure I wanted to stay. In the daylight, this village seemed familiar enough. The houses were the same. The clothes were the same. Even the war chief spoke in an accent that reminded me of my teacher, Dominie Burns.

But things can look different at night — they certainly seemed different in these new surroundings.

I lay awake and listened to the chirp of crickets outside. When I was small, there were nights like this, down by the lake, where Mother and I captured fireflies and watched them glow in our hands. Over the past summer, on hot nights when the moon shone on the water, I would look down at my reflection in the lake, and sometimes I thought I could see her looking back at me, offering a firefly, cupped in her hand. Water can be like that. So can glass.

In the darkness of Good Spirit's home, I listened to the night sounds, but I didn't dare look at the window. They can be mysterious things — windows. You can look at them in different ways and see different things. Look at the window itself and see a pane of glass in a frame; look beyond and see what is outside; or focus your eyes to see the reflection of what is inside the room.

But there in that bed in the dark, I was scared that maybe if I looked at this window, I would witness something else again: a world where those who have died watch us from the darkness.

"Father?"

He shifted in the bed beside me. "Yes, Jacob?"

"Do you believe in ghosts?"

"No, son," he mumbled to the wall.

"So you don't think Mother's spirit is with us?"

He rolled over to face me.

"She's resting in peace, son. Your mother was a good woman and she rests in peace."

"And baby Charlotte too?"

"Yes, Charlotte too," he said. He plumped up the

pillow, then sighed as he flopped back down.

"They're all together in heaven — Mother and Charlotte and my other brothers and sisters?"

"That's right."

The crickets chirped outside, but I still did not want to look at the window.

"What if there's another world, full of ghosts?"

"There are no ghosts." His voice trailed sleepily.

"Henry Ecker said something about what these people believe. The Iroquois, I mean. He said their spirits go on a journey to be with their family and friends in the afterlife."

Father turned his head, "Yes, the Haudenosaunee have a different belief." We both lay there, staring up at the ceiling. "Goodnight," he said at last.

Frogs out there too, along with crickets. And in the distance somewhere, the hoot of an owl.

"What if he's right?"

"Whu . . . ?"

"Henry Ecker. Mother's spirit could be with us still. She would be watching over us. Is that what they really believe? What does Mountain Lion say?"

"These are things he won't talk about — not with outsiders."

"You're not an outsider. You're his *friend.*"

"I am not Haudenosaunee."

"But you don't believe that, do you? Don't believe in ghosts?"

"No, son." His voice drifted off.

I looked at the window then. I could see fireflies out there in the dark, and I told myself they were only fireflies. Just fireflies. That's all.

* * *

I woke up to sunshine pouring through the window. We joined Mountain Lion, Good Spirit and his mother at the breakfast table. Good Spirit was dressed in a shirt, trousers and moccasins. The three of them spoke to Father in their language, and I could make out the words *Jacob* and *Ronhnhí:io*. I tried saying his name to myself again: *Loon-hee-yo*.

Good Spirit gave me a big smile.

"You'll stay with Ronhnhí:io today," Father said. "You're to teach each other your language."

"How long will we be here?"

"Until we've finished the General's business."

* * *

And so we taught each other. Good Spirit learned English faster than I picked up Mohawk.

"What do today, Tchay-cub?"

"Take me hunting?"

"Hun . . . ting?"

"Yes. For food."

I brought my thumbs to my temples and spread my fingers to imitate a deer's antlers. Then I made the motion of a bow and arrow, and the deer dead. Then I pretended to eat.

"Hun–ting," he said, pleased with a new word. "Why hunting? We eat chicken. Pig good."

"We eat those at home too. When are you going to show me how the Haudenosaunee *really* live?" *Haudenosaunee* was one of the few words I had learned.

We found a compromise. He gave me a fishing pole and we hiked up the river. I stripped off my shirt and shoes and loved squishing my toes in the cool mud.

* * *

That day led to a third, and the third to a fourth. On the morning of the fifth day, Mr. Willcocks was well enough to come to Mohawk Village, and the General's negotiations could begin in earnest. That was the day Good Spirit finally took me out to hunt in the woods. His grandfather had given him a musket with grooves scored into the barrel. He was very proud of it and could use it with deadly accuracy. When the shadows lengthened, we headed back toward the village with a brace of jackrabbits and three squirrels slung over our shoulders.

We had wandered far and the light was fading. Good Spirit stopped in the middle of the path and held up his hand for silence.

I heard it then, wafting over the still air of a

summer evening. The pounding drums. Then eerie cries. Voices. A wild song. He turned to me with his eyes bright.

"We war Yankees!" he said.

"*You're* a warrior?"

He shook his head, then rolled his hand, like a wheel moving forward.

"Soon?"

He nodded eagerly. "Yes. Soon."

We hurried through the woods and past the farms where the moon shone down on fields of beans and corn and squash. We followed the drumming and singing and we saw the light of a big bonfire in the heart of the village.

The people had gathered there. Good Spirit and I made our way past the wailing singers and pounding drummers, to where the men danced. Mountain Lion moved his hands, pretending to grab something. He flashed his knife. Another warrior held a club in one hand and a knife in the other and whirled his arms. Most dancers were stripped down to breechcloths, but two stood out in European clothes. Father had removed his shoes, and his feet stamped quickly and lightly the war dance of his boyhood. I had never seen him do this before.

And none the worse for four days in a sickbed, Mr. Willcocks shuffled his boots about as he tried to imitate the warriors. Then he gave it up. He put his hands down to his sides, straightened his back and his feet skipped and lifted in an Irish step dance. The women and children cheered him on.

I turned to say something to Good Spirit, but he was gone. There he was, among the others, leaping and twisting, a skinny body among the muscle.

One dancer whirled and leapt and shrieked to the sky. He thrust his arms to stab and slash the air. The others followed him as he circled the fire, and the women and children parted before him as he danced his way down the road. His scream could curdle milk, and the warriors answered with screams of their own. He danced by me, but his eyes never met mine. They glared at something unseen, something distant. I stepped back in fear of his power, his rage. With a shock I recognized him: Mr. Norton, on his way to war.

Under Attack

October 1812

"Where is your Father?" Mr. Norton asks a third time. He folds his arms and waits, and the others watch me.

"A prisoner," I say at last.

"You were there?" He looks back down the road toward Queenston.

I nod.

"How many soldiers do the Yankees have?"

"I don't know. Seemed like thousands!" Is that right? Maybe only hundreds? More than I've ever seen.

Mr. Norton translates what I've said. Some of the men grumble. Then he turns back to me. "Were our brothers among the Yankees?" He means the Haudenosaunee who live on the other side of the river: were there any among the bluecoats?

I shake my head. "Just army. Some militia."

The warriors talk quietly among themselves, then one man steps into the centre of the circle. I did not learn enough Mohawk during the summer to follow his talk. He points back toward the river and up the Heights. Some men mutter in agreement; others shake their heads. Most turn to Mr. Norton and he watches me.

"Have they taken the high ground?" he asks.

"Yes. And the town. They're everywhere." Control my voice. "They've taken many prisoners. And the cannon." The grumbling around me grows louder. I take a deep breath to steady my voice so the words come out flat. "General Brock is dead."

The grumbling stops.

Mr. Norton says, "You know this for certain?"

"I saw."

I look to Good Spirit, but he stares straight ahead. Mountain Lion rises to his feet and talks, pointing to me and to Good Spirit and clasping his hands — we are together now. With one big sweep of his arm, he gestures down the road toward the enemy. He squats down again, while the voices of others growl and grind like a mill wheel. Others take their turn to speak, and everyone listens. *The best leader,* Father once told me, *is not the one who persuades people to his point of view. He's the one in whose presence people find it easiest to arrive at the truth.*

Those who wish to talk have their say. When all fall silent once more, Mr. Norton speaks again. He pauses, and without another word, he stalks through the circle, crosses the road and heads up a path toward the Heights. Mountain Lion and Good Spirit rise and follow. So do others.

What to do? Take the road or the path? In half an hour, this road could bring me to Mrs. Lovelace's house and safety — warming myself by the fireplace with a bowl of barley soup and bread smothered in butter and dripping with honey. Or follow the deer trail into the forest where the wet branches slash the cold into my clothes. A victorious enemy waits on the Heights. Can I face that again?

I rise to my feet and follow the Mohawk into the forest and up the slope. I haven't a weapon. I can find one. Can I find my courage?

* * *

The distant sound rumbles as if it comes from deep in the ground itself, but it's not the ground; it's the Niagara River where the ground falls away. The Falls are behind us, but I can sense their power even up here on the Heights. When we climbed the path, the river lay far to our left. Now it's below the precipice to our right. Mr. Norton has led us in a big half-circle so that we have sneaked up on our enemy from behind. They're out there somewhere, the blue-coats. And Father. And Eli.

A warrior has given me a weapon — one of those trade muskets with the short barrels that Father and I hauled to Mohawk Village. We trot alongside Mountain Lion and the other warriors. A command from Mr. Norton and we spread out across the fields.

Bluecoats in the distance — a scouting party or a skirmish line. They fire at us, then run for their lives. Good Spirit chirps his war cry, high and sweet among the harsh shrieks of the older warriors. Those bluecoats sure can run! They flee for the safety of a battle line that stretches along a snake-rail fence that edges the Heights, hundreds of uniforms dark against the yellow trees. A big man in a cocked hat waves his sword and the line turns to face us, raising their muskets.

Mr. Norton shouts in Mohawk. I take my cue from Mountain Lion and fling myself to the ground and bury my face in the wheat stubble. First, the crackle of musket fire, then angry hornets whiz over our heads. Good Spirit grins at me. He rises to one knee and squints as he aims. The musket barks. I sight down the barrel. What if Eli is there? No, he's guarding the prisoners. *Is* he?

The warriors shriek their battle cries, and I give our secret call, mine and Eli's, then listen for his reply, but the only response is the crackle of another volley. I squeeze the trigger. The musket slams into my shoulder.

Mr. Norton waves us on toward the trees at the edge of the Heights. Another volley snaps the twigs and cracks the trunks. No one has been hit. A miracle. Or maybe just a better way to fight this enemy.

Mr. Norton motions Good Spirit and me to stay, then slips over the escarpment and into the brush with Mountain Lion and the most experienced warriors. They creep forward toward the enemy and fire at them from the bushes below the lip of the Heights. Good Spirit and I are safe here. We stare out across the plain below.

He pokes my arm and points to the north. Below the Heights, a line of red moves like a caterpillar along the road from Fort George — miles away, but approaching steadily. It's the redcoat army from Fort George, in much bigger numbers than the troops who joined General Brock's attack this morning. Can Mr. Norton, Mountain Lion and the others contain the bluecoats long enough for this force to arrive?

If the bluecoats don't push back our little group, the British will trap them against the cliffs, and they know it. Across the field, the big man with the sword waves the blue line forward — straight for the woods where Good Spirit and I have been ordered to wait. One section of their line stops and raises muskets, while the rest keep coming at us with fixed bayonets. Smoke billows and bullets whip through the trees.

Good Spirit leaps up like a jackrabbit and runs.

I chase after him, deeper into the woods. Another volley. We fling ourselves to the ground and the lead slices into the leaves. Run. Run. Run. Duck. Up. Run again.

I stumble toward a huge oak and slump to the ground, gasping for breath. Good Spirit follows, but he stands with his back against the tree, his legs apart. A squirrel scolds us. Good Spirit stares into the trees, his eyes wide.

"You safe?"

Slowly his back slides down the tree, but his feet don't move. He squats and stares. Tears roll down his cheeks.

"I . . . I . . . " he murmurs. He cannot meet my eyes.

And then I smell it. I look at him a moment. "That happens," I say softly. "It happened to me. This morning. It happens to soldiers."

"Not warriors," he mumbles. "Not Mohawk. I shame me. Shame Grandfather." And the squirrel natters at us again. I poke my head around the trunk. The blue line has stopped at last. I can't see any warriors, but I hear their shouts.

I turn back to Good Spirit. His head droops and his prized musket lies at his feet. I offer a handful of wet leaves, and he doesn't meet my eyes while he takes them. I turn away and study the enemy line once more. Where is everybody? Mr. Norton?

Mountain Lion? I look back at Good Spirit as he draws up his trousers.

"No one's ever going to know," I say. He looks up and smiles gratefully. "Come on. Let's find the others."

Good Spirit still has his musket. Somewhere in my flight back there, I threw mine away. I'm the one who should be ashamed.

* * *

Through the forest, an angry voice barks words I cannot understand. The land slopes downhill, and there on the dry ground beneath a tree, Mr. Norton argues with warriors who sit and wait for their turn to speak. When he sees us approach, Mr. Norton's face lights up. Mountain Lion rises to his feet and smiles. Mr. Norton gestures toward Good Spirit and puts an arm over his shoulder while pointing an accusing finger at the others.

I don't remember seeing many of these men during our attack. Did they stay here, well back of the fighting? Is Good Spirit being praised for his bravery?

Mountain Lion approaches his grandson and takes his hands and places them on his chest. I cannot tell which of them is more proud.

Smashing the Enemy

October 1812

The bluecoats have returned to the snake-rail fence and we've slipped back into the woods nearby. The sky has cleared, and across the fields, bayonets shine in the sun where the redcoats assemble. Here in the woods, we have no bayonets and no sun.

On the other side of a fallen log, Good Spirit fires, then slips through the brush toward me. Our eyes meet.

I'm good.

Me too.

Warriors at last.

I have found my trade musket. My powder remains dry. I crouch beside the trunk of a beech tree to load and fire. Beyond the fallen log, Mr. Norton stalks through the underbrush and speaks to Mountain Lion and Good Spirit; then it's my turn.

"How are you, Master Gibson? Do you have enough cartridges?"

"I'm almost out. What's going on? Sir?"

He lifts the flap of my cartridge box and checks for himself.

"Slow down your fire," he says. "You'll need these later." He pulls three cartridges from his own box and slides them into place in mine.

"Are we going to attack?"

"I'm waiting to hear from General Sheaffe. In the meantime, we pin them down."

He passes me a wooden canteen. I don't think I've ever been so thirsty; nor has water ever tasted so good — in spite of the grit of gunpowder. "Not too much," he warns. I return the bottle, and he grips my shoulder before slipping away. "Stay strong."

Beyond the next tree, I hear him talking again — still the same calm voice, only this time in Mohawk.

But now there's another voice farther into the woods. "Norton?" it calls. "Is that you? You're the devil to find on an afternoon stroll." I recognize the voice. "Everything aright? Right as roosters!"

Mr. Willcocks! At last, someone from home. I signal to Good Spirit and Mountain Lion, then creep through the brush toward the voice.

"General Sheaffe," he shouts above the gunfire, "will strike presently. His compliments, and he commends you to keep up the pressure. Good work, Captain. How many men have you?"

I can see them now through the leaves: Mr. Norton

in his feathers and leather; Mr. Willcocks in his green coat and high boots.

"A hundred warriors," Mr. Norton replies, "and one boy — one of yours."

"Mine?"

"Young Gibson."

"Gibson? *Jacob* Gibson?" I can't hear Mr. Norton's reply, but Mr. Willcocks booms, "What the blazes is he doing here? His father will have something to say about that!"

I steal back to my hiding place behind the tree. When I apprenticed at Mr. Willcocks's newspaper, I sometimes made mistakes. Well, I *often* made mistakes, especially in the first weeks. I would mix up my Ps and Qs, or I would put too much water on the paper. Back then, I sometimes wished I could hide so he wouldn't find out. He'll never find me here. Maybe.

"Jacob Gibson?" he shouts. "Jacob, where are you?"

Instead of his usual walking stick, Mr. Willcocks pushes his way through the underbrush with a long rifle. The bullets zing above him. Two pistols stick in his belt. I know those pistols. They were used in a duel once, then later against William, Henry and Mr. McKenney. Do I stand up to meet him? Not with these bullets whizzing by. But the big man attracts musket fire as he slashes his way through the brush. If I continue to hide, I'll put him in danger.

"Hello, Mr. Willcocks." I try to smile.

He jumps back, startled, but he quickly recovers. "What are *you* doing here? Does your father know?"

His top hat flies from his head and lands on the moss. He picks it up and pokes his finger through a bullet hole in the crown. He crouches beside me and ducks his head. I smell alcohol.

"Father's over there," I say.

He scowls at his ruined hat and snaps, "Well, he'll certainly have something to say about this. I have half a mind to take you by the ear and haul you . . . " He looks up. "Robert? He's over *there*?" He points to the enemy lines.

"A prisoner."

He studies me a moment. "How do you know?"

"I saw. This morning. Eli's there too."

"*You* were there this morning?" He tilts his hat on the back of his head and scratches his scalp. "Just what have you been up to, young Gibson?"

"I came with Father. I hid in his wagon and fought in the battle."

"Well, we'll just have to get you out of here — to someplace safe."

"No, sir."

"I beg your pardon?"

What have I just said? It came out instinctively. I've never defied an adult before — and certainly never one with such a forceful personality. "I'm staying here, Mr. Willcocks."

"You'll do as I say. Now, get to the rear."

"No, sir." He stares at me as if he can't believe what I'm saying. "You're not my boss any more."

"I'm sure that your father would delegate his authority to me, young man, so let's have no more of this kind of talk."

"My duty's here, sir. With Mr. Norton. With my comrades."

A few feet over, Good Spirit scrambles back up onto his log again, taunting the enemy. Then he leaps for cover and rolls over the rocky ground as the bullets whine overhead. He comes to a rest beside us.

Mr. Willcocks looks at Good Spirit, then back at me.

"What is this? The Children's Crusade?"

"Don't worry about us, sir. We're safe here."

He shakes his head and shrugs. He pulls a whisky flask from his boot and offers it to me. I shake my head. He holds the flask toward Good Spirit, who pushes his hand away. Mr. Willcocks shrugs again and takes a gentlemanly sip, then tucks the flask back into his boot.

"Well, boys," Mr. Willcocks says as he picks up his rifle again, "count me among the comrades."

* * *

Mr. Willcocks loves to talk. I've heard him give speeches that go on for two hours, and I've seen him keep a dinner table full of grown-ups transfixed with his stories. So why should he be any different in the heat of a battle?

"The thing about it is" — he says as he loads his rifle once more — "our late-lamented General Brock was bold" — he slips the ramrod back into place — "but too reckless by half." He half-cocks the flint. "General Sheaffe, on the other hand, may have none of Brock's charisma." He shoulders his rifle and aims down the barrel. "But he knows better than to charge up a" — the flint snaps against the steel and the rifle fires — "cliff."

Good Spirit and Mountain Lion don't understand all of this, but he chatters away as if we were all part of his audience.

"Slow and steady. Eh? And methodical. That's how to win this battle."

I rise behind the tree to take my shot. A bank of smoke clings to the ground like a fog.

"You fellows have done a capital job keeping those people penned up. Simply capital! Now that the army has arrived, well, we'll just roll them out like dough and bake them in a pie."

Mr. Willcocks might be right: the secret of winning is to wait until everything is ready, and now the time has come. In the field far to our right, drums beat, orders bawl, battle flags poke above eddies of smoke. The fog lifts for a moment, and a redcoat army moves forward — hundreds of white trousers stepping in unison. Hundreds of muskets levelled at once. A deafening roar of a volley, then the machine marches forward again.

"Tallyho!" says Mr. Willcocks. "Now, you lads stay right here."

"Where are you going?"

"Why, to join the attack of course."

"We're coming too."

"No, no, lads. You do what you do best. Keep firing from the woods. It's going to get messy out there."

"I need to save Father. And Eli."

"Jacob, they'll be safer if they don't have to worry about you. And so will I. Now be a good lad and stay right here." He jumps over the rock and disappears into the smoke.

Good Spirit and I look at each other, then dash right along behind. The fog lifts and lowers in pockets of light and darkness. Here it swirls as a musket fires. There it billows with the roar of another volley. Bullets whiz. The most terrifying sound of all is not the buzz of those angry hornets, but the shriek of the Mohawk warriors, unseen in the haze. Figures appear and disappear. Some lie on the grass, and the fog does not hide the blood and shattered flesh. I just need to follow Mr. Willcocks — or find him again.

Over there: he and Mountain Lion fight side by side. Mr. Willcocks dodges the thrust of a bayonet, then smashes a man in the face with the butt of his rifle. He pulls out a pistol and shoots another bluecoat in the chest. Mountain Lion swings down his war club, and the man moves no more. Then they rush farther into the smoke.

I turn to reassure Good Spirit, but he needs no help from me. His face is set and hard. He clicks the flintlock on his musket and aims into the melee.

The redcoat army has reached the fence and the enemy falls back. A bluecoat officer waves a white flag, but no one seems to notice. Another volley of musketry and his white flag is lost in swirling clouds of sulphur. Among the shrieks and gunfire, a deeper sound rises from below. The river is down there somewhere, and the cliff up ahead. I'm running out of space to find Father and Eli.

"Jake!"

His face appears white in the smoke. He stands with a splintered musket in his hand. His blue eyes widen further as he looks past my shoulder. He raises the useless stock above his face to shield a blow. A figure hurtles past me and a club crashes down. Eli staggers to the ground and his eyes roll back. Buckskin and feathers are upon him. A knife flashes.

I hurl myself at the buckskin and we both tumble over. I know this man. Mountain Lion. "No!" I scramble to my feet and fling myself to the ground where Eli lies. "Stop!"

Mountain Lion rushes toward us, his knife poised. I'm backed up against Eli's head and I raise my hands in surrender. If Mountain Lion doesn't recognize me, I'm dead. I stare at him steadily, my eyes looking for recognition in his.

"Tako'skó:wa!" I raise my voice as loud and clear as I can with the rasp that is in my throat. But my voice is strong after all. Strong enough to stop a scalping knife.

Crows

October 1812

I shield Eli with my body. The battle rages around, but no one pays attention to two figures lying on the ground, two among so many. Eli has been knocked out cold, and I lie equally still, turning my face to the wet leaves and the splatters of blood. His chest rises and falls beneath me. Footsteps rush past. Gunfire. Shouts of warriors. Screams of pain. The shrieks of grown men who plead for mercy. And worst: the silence that follows.

I hold Eli tight. We were the same size when he saved me from drowning in the river. His sister, Mina, once teased us, "You boys ain't got enough meat on them bones to feed a crow."

I lift my head. On the top rail of the fence, a big black bird watches me, tilting its head to consider its next move. It hops to the ground.

"Go away!"

The crow flaps lazily back to the fence. I sit up and rest Eli's head in my lap. I've done this before, the night I knocked him out with Father's cleaning spirits to keep him from getting into trouble. I take the tail of my nightshirt to wipe away some of the blood and dirt. He moans with pain, but his eyes stay closed. One eye is swelling and I scoop some leaves and place them over the bruise.

Around us, the dead and wounded lie among the debris. A dead man stretches a white hand toward us and stares at me, a bloody patch on his head — scalped. The crow glides from the fence and settles on the man's shoulder.

The bang of the musketry and boom of cannon have ceased. No war cries or victims' shrieks. But the wounded moan and the crows caw. Another sound floats through the fog from the edge of the Heights.

"Jacob! Jacob Gibson!"

"Father!" But my throat stings from gunpowder and my voice cracks.

Through the smoke comes a dark shape, a familiar stoop in his shoulders. I saw that shape running into the dark this morning. Only this morning? I call again and he changes direction, climbing stiffly over the rail fence. I raise Eli's head and rest it gently on the ground, but when I try to rise to my feet, my legs have gone numb and I stumble forward into Father's arms.

"My boy . . . My boy . . . "

I cry into his coat and hold him as tight as I can, and his arms wrap around me. His shoulders shake.

I open my eyes. Mr. Willcocks climbs over the fence. He has lost his hat and his coat is torn. He watches us a moment, then kneels beside Eli. I close my eyes again. Squeeze harder. Feel Father's chest against me, warm, alive. And we stay like that for a long time.

* * *

Mr. Willcocks wraps his cravat around Eli's head and over one eye. "Was he alone? Where's his father?"

I shake my head. I don't know.

"McCabe was with him when I was captured," Father says. "He asked his captain to put Eli on prisoner detail."

I scan the bodies that lie sprawled across the field. Mr. McCabe is a huge man — he'd be easy to spot even on the battlefield. I don't see him here.

"We'll find him." Father rests his hand on my shoulder. "Everything will be . . . will be . . . "

"Right as roosters," mutters Mr. Willcocks. Eli's eye flutters open slowly, then jerks wide with terror. "Rest easy, young man," Mr. Willcocks soothes. "We're all friends here."

Eli raises a hand to the bandage, feels gingerly around the wound, then his good eye widens as if looking at something none of the rest of us can see. He says nothing.

A redcoat officer picks his way through the carnage and calls to Father, "All American militia are to give their parole. We will convey them back across the river." This is good news. It means they must promise not to fight again.

Father says to the redcoat, "This young one can't give his parole."

"See for yourself, Lieutenant," Mr. Willcocks adds. "He's not talking — can promise nothing."

Father lowers his voice. He thinks he's out of Eli's hearing. "His father is missing. Maybe among the dead."

I can't hear what the officer says, but Father replies, "We'll take him to Newark. He'll be in our custody."

Another officer on horseback rides up. "Mr. Willcocks? And Mr. Gibson? General Sheaffe's compliments, gentlemen, and he requests your audience along with Captain Norton."

"When?" asks Mr. Willcocks.

"Now, sir."

"Can you give us a moment?" Father asks.

"General Sheaffe requests your *immediate* attention."

Father turns to me. "Stay here," he says.

I am so tired, so numb, this seems like the easiest instruction in the world. Just sit here while Eli stares off into space. His fingers search absently through the grass. He picks something up and stares at it dully. It's an acorn. He places it carefully in the cloth haversack he wears at his hip, then stares off again.

The gun smoke drifts and lifts like a curtain to reveal things I don't want to look at any more. The crows are everywhere. Hundreds of them. An army of crows. Up along the snake-rail fence, a group of Mohawk have gathered in a circle, their heads down. I watch them a moment, then watch the crows along the fence again. Some crows wait patiently for the living to leave them to their dinner. Others, bolder, spread their wings and glide down to the grass.

The Mohawk still stand there. Mr. Norton is not among them. He's gone to see General Sheaffe. Father too. And Mr. Willcocks. What can that be about? The warriors stand with their heads bowed and their shoulders slumped. One of them raises his head and his arms to the sky, but there is no sky, only the lifting fog of war. There's Mountain Lion. He kneels on one leg, bending over something I cannot see. Where's Good Spirit? Something is wrong. What is wrong? I've got a bad feeling about this.

"Eli, you've got to stay here. Understand? Just don't move. I'll be back."

Every muscle in my body aches and complains at having to move again, but I keep focused on that group of warriors. Mountain Lion gently touches something there in the grass.

I don't dare look — just stare at the ground. An army shako. A broken sabre. Cartridge paper, scorched and blackened. Dead leaves, trampled into the mud. A musket. A boy. I kneel beside him. Mountain Lion gently touches his eyelids, and the brown eyes close. The Mohawk speak words I don't understand, and I don't listen. I reach out to brush away the trickle of blood that runs from the corner of Ronhnhí:io's mouth, but Mountain Lion motions with his hand that I am not to touch. If a person's spirit hovers nearby, is Ronhnhí:io watching us now? His body chills in the autumn air.

A crow hops on the grass nearby. I pick up an acorn and raise my arm. The crow tilts its head and watches me with intelligent eyes, and I put the acorn away. The crow looks this way and that, unconcerned, among the legs of the warriors who stand around Good Spirit. With his eyes closed, my friend looks as if he is sleeping.

How will your people send you on your journey, Ronhnhí:io? I don't know what your burial customs are, but if Mountain Lion takes you home, I will go with you to the village. This I promise to do. Father will understand.

But from behind me comes a new sound. The *trrrill* of a drum, followed by the moans of men who know what it means. A rattle of buckles and bayonets and the shuffle of thousands of feet. With a collective groan, a thousand men rise from their rest and assemble on the road.

Tap. Tap. Tap-tap-tap, beats the drum.

I glance behind me. Eli! He's been picking up acorns and stuffing them in his haversack, all the while staring into the distance. But now he rises to his feet.

"Eli, wait!"

If he hears me, he doesn't show it. He turns slowly toward the column of soldiers that snakes its way down the slope.

"Eli!"

I glance back at the warriors. Mountain Lion's face had been drawn away into some inner world, but now he looks at me calmly, then nods for me to go. I take one last look at Good Spirit. A white rib pokes out from the blood and flesh. That is not how I want to remember. No. I study his sleeping face once more, then turn and run to catch up to Eli. "Wait, Eli. We're supposed to stay here."

But he puts one foot in front of the other, left, right, left, right, and his eye stares at the back of the man in front of him. I grab his arm and try to pull him aside. He turns and looks at me with his unbandaged eye, but there's no recognition. He keeps marching.

"Help me," I say to the soldier behind me. "We're supposed to stay here." But the soldier looks at me blankly.

"Keep moving, there!" shouts an officer. "Close up those ranks." And I fall in place beside Eli as we trudge down the hill.

Fire

October 1812

Night falls early and the darkness grows as we march through the village. Not marching, exactly, in spite of the tapping of the drum: a tired shuffle of a thousand men.

We pass the Secord house where a light glows behind the curtains. Here is the spot where I left Solomon. The wagon has been smashed by a cannonball, but there's no trace of blood. Here is where I saw the fox. More than just farmyard chickens for her to feast on tonight.

I might have saved Good Spirit if I'd stayed with him. But then Eli would have been killed. What could I have done? What should I have done?

"Steady over there," calls a sergeant. "Keep to the road." I wrap my arm around Eli's waist and support his weight while I point him toward home. He stares at the ground. The moon rises on the far side of the river.

"Gibson! Is that you?"

"And who's that? Not the Turd Boy too!"

"And just when I thought we'd rid the province of Yankees."

William and Henry emerge in the darkness. Tonight, even William looks dirty.

"You on prisoner detail?" I ask.

"Yes," William grumbles. "Again."

"But we got to fight after all," Henry adds. "Great charge, eh? Never had so much fun in my life!"

"What about *him*?" William nods. Eli keeps staring ahead as we walk.

"He fought too," I reply.

In the moonlight, William's catlike eyes watch, assess. "With *them*?" he says.

"Didn't he swear allegiance?" asks Henry.

"His father certainly did," William responds. "No end of trouble getting him to do it."

"Did the father fight against us too?" Henry asks me, then he turns to William. "I knew we couldn't trust them. Good riddance."

"Where is the father?" William asks me. When I don't reply, he continues, "So . . . if Turd Boy is in the Yankee militia, he shouldn't be here, then. He should have given his parole." After a pause, he says, "But like father like son, I guess. Can't trust his word."

Henry growls, "I hope he doesn't take as long as his father to swear an oath. He'll be with us all winter."

And then he turns to Eli. "Isn't that right, Turd Boy? Turd Boy! I'm talking to you."

Eli looks at the grass as he walks.

"Save it for later," William tells Henry.

"We should just let the Iroquois handle them," Henry mutters. "Did you see? Some of those Yankees were so scared, they jumped off the cliffs rather than face the tomahawk." He turns to look back at the soldiers coming down the road. "What will we do with all these prisoners? Can't put all of them in jail."

And William adds, "How will we feed them?"

Henry shrugs. "If it was up to me, we'd just let them go. The Iroquois would handle it in short order."

William turns to me. "We're not *guarding* prisoners, really. More like *protecting* them."

Henry adds, "Did you see how the Iroquois fought? I'm going to get myself one of those scalping knives!" He reaches for the air above Eli's hair, making a slashing motion with his other hand.

Eli keeps walking, keeps staring down.

"You leave him alone, Henry," I say. "He's under my protection."

"Ah, Gibson," William tuts. "I had such hopes for you."

Henry studies Eli, then turns to William. "Do you suppose it's treason?"

"What do you mean?" I ask.

"Turd Boy's a subject of His Majesty, but he fought for the other side."

"Eli's an American."

Then from far behind us, through the rattle of equipment and the squish of boots in the mud, a voice calls, "Jacob!" William and Henry look at me. The voice calls again, a little closer. "Jacob Gibson?"

"Here, Father! Up the road."

I seize Eli with both hands and pull him to the side of the road.

"We'll deal with you later," says Henry as he and William slip into the flow of soldiers filing by. Through the moonlight looms a horse — Solomon, drawing a farm wagon. Father sits on the seat between two wounded soldiers. I leave Eli at the side of the road and wrap my arms around Solomon's neck. He raises and lowers his head and nuzzles my hair.

The two soldiers move to the back of the wagon, and Eli and I climb up. Behind us, a long lump wrapped in a linen sheet takes most of the room. None of the soldiers touches it.

* * *

If I just keep talking. I won't have time to think. "Father?"

He straightens his back. "Yes, Jacob."

"Will Eli stay in my room?" I nudge Eli to get a reaction, but he stares at the red glow in the night sky.

"We'll make a trundle bed. In the kitchen."

"With Ginger?" Father nods his head, but says nothing. "Ginger's sure going to be happy to see you, Eli. Eli?" I nudge him again. The reins hang loose in Father's hands. I reach over and take them.

"Do I need to feed Solomon?" Father jerks his head and opens his eyes. "When we get home, I mean." He looks at me, trying to understand. "Feed Solomon."

He nods yes.

"Maybe Eli can go to bed first — while I take care of Solomon."

Neither of them responds. Then Father says, "First we must deliver the General."

I look back. Some soldiers lean against one another. Others sleep bolt upright where they sit. But no one touches the figure wrapped in linen. General Brock.

"Where will we take him?"

"Government House."

Is General Brock's spirit nearby? Are all the dead marching with us on their way home? Don't think about that — just keep talking. In the distance, the low-hanging clouds glow red and orange.

"Why is the sky that colour?"

"Fire," says Father. When he was a boy, the whole Mohawk Valley must have glowed like this — when he and his neighbours left the burning ruins of their homes to flee to Canada, the rebels in pursuit. And then I understand. Our battle was not fought only at Queenston; buildings are burning in Newark too, and their flames light up the sky, the way Eli's tannery did that night last winter when someone torched the vat shed.

"What caused the fire?"

"Heated shot. From Fort Niagara."

"How do you know?"

"General Sheaffe told us."

Fort Niagara stands like a stone castle across the river from our town. On our side, Fort George is made of logs. What chance would it have against red-hot cannonballs? Newark is built of wood too.

"Our house? Is it . . . ?"

Father turns to look at me. "We will find out when we've finished our duty."

"Is Ginger going to be safe?"

But he does not reply.

* * *

I have lost Good Spirit. I have found Eli, but it's as if I've lost him again. What if I have lost Ginger too? Yesterday morning, I was crabby and impatient. "We're going away for just one night, girl. Settle down!" But she barked and whined as we pulled away and, when we turned onto King Street, she gave one plaintive howl that carried all the way past the courthouse.

Did she think she was saying goodbye to me forever? Do dogs foresee these things? If something has happened to her, I'll never forgive myself.

The stench of woodsmoke hangs in the air, and something stronger — sweet but gut-wrenching: the smell of burnt wool and burnt bacon. Or is it burnt dog? We pass Fort George, where soldiers use the flaming ruins as giant campfires as they make their beds for the night. We pull up to Government House, and Eli stays on the seat while Father and I help the soldiers carry General Brock's body. As we pass through the doorway, the sheet falls away and the gold braid of his epaulette shines in the candlelight.

Father and I rejoin Eli. Solomon pulls us down King Street, his pace picking up as we head for home. Bricks lie on the ground at the Dunwoody house, where a cannonball has knocked away the chimney. The paint on the Masonic lodge has been scorched black. From the flaming, flickering rubble that yesterday was the courthouse, a black rectangle silhouettes against the red sky like a giant tombstone. I stare at the precision of it, then realize it is the oak door of one of the jail cells. The walls have burned down around it. Mr. McKenney won't keep any prisoners there now!

Eli and I used to tell each other the same joke,

over and over: "I know a man with a wooden leg named McKenney." "What's the name of his other leg?" I study Eli's face now. Do I try our old joke on him — see if he responds? But no one's in the mood for silly humour.

Solomon turns onto Prideaux Street. Will he find a stable and food . . . or ashes, smoke and a dead dog? A sharp bark of welcome. More barks. Ginger gallops up the road and I leap off the seat to meet her down in the mud. She scampers and twirls and rests her paws on my shoulders as she licks my face.

She runs circles in the grass and when she comes back, Eli stands beside me on the road. His eye still has that dazed, faraway look. Ginger scrambles back and bowls him over, and he just lies there in the road while she licks his face. And still he says nothing.

Eli's Silence

October 1812

I'm lost in the fog. The sounds of battle grow near — bursts of muskets, shouts of orders, screams of the wounded, Indian war cries. I steal forward through the woods, every step tentative. The enemy hunts me as I hunt him. His musket cracks. The ball whizzes by my head and smacks into a tree.

I turn and raise my firearm. Through the smoke, Good Spirit stands in a patch of ferns. There is no blood, no bullet hole. He smiles and motions me to come to him. I lower my weapon. Now General Brock and Colonel Macdonell stand behind him. They wave me forward, but I shake my head. They fade into the mist and fly away as crows.

A man remains standing in the ferns and the fog — a big man, as round as he is tall, with massive shoulders and a short neck. His eyes are bright blue, the same colour as Eli's. "Take care of my boy," he says, and he reaches out with a warm sponge as he scrubs my face.

A wet dog tongue on my cheek. Ginger. What is she doing here?

Wait. I'm downstairs in our kitchen. Eli sleeps beside me, curled up with his hands covering his face. I remember now. Father removed his bandages and washed his wounds while I pulled out the trundle bed. We slept here with Ginger beside the hearth. Now she nuzzles Eli, but he doesn't wake up.

"Let him be, girl." We're alone in the house with the ticking of the clock. I slip on a shirt and pull up my suspenders, grab my jacket, and Ginger and I head out the door where the cold sun shines through the pall of smoke that still hangs in the air. I must find Mina to tell her about her brother.

Wisps of smoke rise from the charred rubble of the courthouse, and a platoon of redcoats picks through the debris and contemplates what to do about the door. Was anyone left behind in the jail? What would have happened if Mr. McKenney's wooden leg caught fire? I can't help it: I picture him running around trying to stamp it out and jamming it into a bucket of water and hissing steam.

In the daylight, the scorch marks on the Masonic lodge stand out black against the whitewashed walls. Did the library survive? Where would we have put the books? Underground in the root cellars, perhaps. But would they survive the mould and damp?

I round the corner to King Street and slam into

someone — bump so hard, I fall backward. I squint up at a silhouette in the October sun.

"Jacob Gibson," says a girl's voice, "you gotta watch where you're going!" She reaches down and helps me to my feet. Her hands are rough-skinned and very strong. Mina McCabe, the very person I was rushing to find. "You got my brother?"

"How'd you know?"

"Master William says."

It's so strange to hear Mina refer to anyone as a *master*, let alone William Dunwoody. She's been working as the Dunwoodys' servant since her family left for the American states, and I don't like to think about that. In fact, I try not to think about Mina at all, but it's hard. I can't keep her out of my dreams — the way she looks in the summer, when her skirts are hitched up and I can see the brown of her ankles and the white of her legs.

She hasn't even bothered to put a coat on, even though the morning is crisp. She wears an apron and a cap, but her black hair spills out over her shoulders.

"How's my little brother?"

"He's whole. But he's not himself, Mina. He hasn't said a word."

"Eli? Usually can't shut him up!"

"He's been through . . . " I don't know what to say. I follow her down Prideaux Street.

"What about Pa?"

"I . . . I don't know, Mina. No one's seen him." It's hard to keep pace with her long strides. "I dreamt about him last night."

"Pa?"

"He came to me. He said, *Take care of my boy.*"

She stops. "In your dream? You sure it was Pa?"

"No one else looks like your father."

She stares out toward the lake. "I dreamt about him too. Last night." She looks at me. "But he didn't say nothing. He just looked at me kinda sad." And she's off again, marching toward our house. When I open the door, Ginger scurries ahead into the kitchen.

"Eli? You awake?" He sits on the trundle bed with one arm around Ginger as she licks his bruised face. His right eye is swollen shut.

"Little brother?" Then Mina gives a cry when she sees his wound. He stares and his good eye brims with tears, but he doesn't move. Mina kneels beside him and wraps her arms around him and she talks so softly and gently, I can't make out what she's saying. Eli just stares at the door with his one good eye.

"Get me water," Mina tells me. "As cold as you can find."

* * *

The lighthouse beam sweeps across the dark water, flashes briefly on the American fort across the river, then moves on to the town behind us. Father says it guides the sailors and fishermen to our harbour. For Eli and me, the lighthouse has been the place to meet and to share secrets. Beyond the ridge, the waves rattle the pebbles. The wind has picked up and our campfire burns fiercely, low to the ground.

Eli sits there with a blanket over his shoulders and head, staring into the fire. Something at the edge of the firelight catches his attention. He rises to his feet.

"Eli?"

He doesn't reply — just walks over, picks something out of the grass and puts it into his haversack. What does he carry in there? When his father ran the tannery, Eli always had a leather bag to collect dog poop to help cure skins into leather. Hope that's not what he's doing now.

"Eli?"

He trudges back to the log and sits down again. If there's something smelly in that bag, Ginger's going to notice first, but she just lies there. Eli fishes around the haversack and an acorn falls out and lands on the ground. He picks it up and stares at it for a long time, then gazes back into the fire and puts the acorn back in the cloth bag.

"Eli, what are you doing with all those acorns?" He's not listening, so we just sit there while the flames pop. "Eli," I say at last, "you've got to come out of this. We're all worried about you." I wait for a response, but I can't tell whether he hears me. "Remember this place? We swore our oath to each other that winter. Right here. Blood brothers." His left eye blinks rapidly. Maybe it's just the campfire smoke. "We used your knife to cut our palms."

He stares into the coals and so I sit across from him and look out at the water. In a few months, the lake will freeze, then it will thaw, and it will freeze again, and I wish I could say we would still be meeting here. I look back to him. "We promised our ultimate loyalty to each other, and we've got to stand by that. Nothing is going to come between us, Eli — not even being on different sides in this war."

Again the lighthouse swings its beam slowly across the black lake.

"Eli, I kept a big secret from you. General Brock sent me on a mission." I wait for his response, but he keeps staring into the fire. "No one was to know about it. Not even you." I hesitate. *Especially* not Eli. "We went to talk with the Haudenosaunee — I mean, the Iroquois. We got them to join the war." His eye is blinking again — not as fast as before, but there's a fear there at the very word *Iroquois*. The fire snaps and crackles. Ginger huffs in her sleep.

"I have a friend in Mohawk Village," I begin. "I *had* a friend. He was killed yesterday." I stare into the fire. "He may be sitting at this campfire with us, but we can't see him." I pull my blanket closer around me. "Eli, I've seen so many dead people these last days. What if there really are ghosts? I'm so scared, I don't know what to do."

I haven't been able to look at his face. A shiver runs up my spine as the wind picks up and billows the yellow flames.

I raise my chin, lift my eyes. Eli looks at me, one eye swollen shut, but the other — his bright blue eye — gazes at me with such kindness and pity that my heart stops racing and I give him a quiet smile.

But still he says nothing.

Funeral March

October 1812

Down the street, someone shouts an order, and the murmuring crowd falls silent. People crane their necks to see. Somewhere across town, a dog barks. A cow moos. I hear these things, but I listen to Eli's silence as I straddle the branch of an oak tree and he sits on the bough below. Then, far down the road, a muffled sound:

Duddle-um. Dum. Da-dum.

The crowd remains hushed. How can so many people make so little noise? On each side of the road, a row of soldiers, militia and Haudenosaunee warriors stands with heads bowed and muskets pointed to the ground. Behind them, people jostle to get a view. There's Mrs. Lovelace and the two girls. George worms her way to the front of the crowd. Her shoulders are straight and she lifts her chin so the sunlight glistens on her tears. She glances to see if anyone is watching her.

Mrs. Lovelace and Abby stay farther back. Soon

Father and Mrs. Lovelace will set their wedding date, and I'm not going to fight that any more. If Father wants to remarry, then maybe it's best not to wait. No use waiting for anything.

And there's Mina. Her face is mostly hidden by her bonnet. Does she know we're up here?

Duddle-um. Dum. Da-dum. Getting closer, louder, but the procession is still far down the road. *Duddle-um. Dum. Da-dum.* Now the fifes play low.

From the fort, a cannon booms. Eli jerks on his perch. He's going to fall onto the people below, but he grabs the branch and steadies himself and looks up to me, frightened.

"All's right, Eli. That's a minute gun." His eyes dart toward the lake, then back at me.

"What's a minute gun?"

I study him closely. He's said something. After *three* days.

"They'll fire it every minute."

"Hush, up there," mutters an old man below us. Eli pays him no attention.

"No one's gonna attack?" he says in a lower voice. He's talking! I ignore the frowns from the people in the street.

"Every minute. No cannonballs. To show respect." He lets that sink in.

"That's nice. Real nice." For three days he hasn't said a word, but at the very moment to be silent, he finds his voice. "What if someone loaded a real cannonball? By mistake, I mean."

This is more like Eli. Faces glare up at me, but I decide to risk a response. "No one's going to do that. There's a truce."

"Or what if they attack now — when you ain't expecting? What if they cross the river right in the middle of this parade?" He says *they* rather than *we* — a good sign.

"Maybe they'll have enough boats this time." I mean it as a joke, but now have I offended him? I'm sure annoying the people beneath this tree.

Boom goes the cannon. He flinches. Then he screws up his face and wipes his nose on his sleeve.

"I don't reckon anyone's got the belly to fight any more. I know I ain't."

"Hush, up there," the old man scolds again.

Duddle-um. Dum. Da-dum.

Major Campbell and the first ranks have reached us now, their feet crunching on the fallen acorns. Behind the soldiers of His Majesty's 41st Regiment of Foot, Lieutenant Colonel Dunwoody leads the Lincoln County militia. The Lincolns never marched well, but today they all hold their heads high.

"There's your pa," says Eli.

Yes, there he is, musket over his shoulder. He looks older than the others. He asked me whether I would like to march beside him, and I thought about it, but someone has to take care of Eli. He's entrusted to my charge. A strange way to guard a prisoner: up here in a tree, watching the cortège go by.

Boom goes the cannon.

Down the road, there's the General's horse, Alfred, led by four grooms, and behind him I can see the two carriages that carry the coffins.

But now there's a rustle and a ruckus below me — in the ranks of the Lincoln County militia.

"Ow!" shouts someone. A man slaps his hand against his cheek.

"Oops," says Eli.

What's he doing? His hand is drawn back and he flings it forward. The militia break ranks as they duck. An object knocks the top hat off one of the marchers.

"We see you, McCabe. Don't think we don't."

"You'll pay for this, Turd Boy."

"Quiet in the ranks!" shouts a sergeant.

There they are among the flinching militiamen: William and Henry. Henry shoves aside the man marching in front of him and strides toward us.

"You there!" the sergeant yells, "get back to your place."

But Henry doesn't stop. He pushes his way through. "We'll let the Iroquois handle you," he yells, "or I'll scalp you myself." Then he stops and claps his hand to his face.

Eli! How many acorns does he have stuffed in that

haversack? There goes another one. He wings it fast and it hits Henry again, this time on the top of his head.

"What are you doing up there?" shouts the old man below us.

"Stop those boys!"

But Eli just laughs. For someone balanced with both feet on a tree limb, he throws hard.

"Eli!"

He searches in his bag for more acorns, but comes up empty-handed. An acorn knocks into the trunk by my head. William. He's fighting back, picking up the acorns from the ground and flinging them at us.

And Eli, he . . .

I can't believe . . .

He hurls the haversack and turns his back on them all, sitting like a bird perched on the oak limb. Then he drops his trousers and waves his white bum at William, at Henry, at the Lincoln County Militia and the whole funeral procession.

"Get him!"

It's not just the old man shouting at us now. Eli!

William stoops to pick up an acorn.

"Eli!"

"Ow!" yelps Eli and then he laughs.

Boom goes the minute gun.

"You'll pay for this, Turd Boy."

Eli pulls up his trousers and scrambles across the branches, as reckless as a squirrel. I follow as fast as

I can. We leap to the ground and run. How we run! Eli buttons his trousers.

So I don't see the big white horse walk by, nor the coffins of General Brock and Colonel Macdonell. The crowd will leave us alone — will follow the procession to the fort — but Eli and I sprint in the opposite direction.

* * *

On King Street, we pause for breath.

"What were you *thinking*!" I don't hide my anger.

"Corn, Slim, they looked so smug and la-de-da."

"What are you talking about?"

"Junior. Lug. They ain't no better'n me."

Junior and Lug. I haven't heard William and Henry called that since Eli left the Canadas.

"What's this got to do with them?"

"Can't stand those two."

I wave my hands in exasperation. "Never mind them."

"Uppity. That's what they are. Uppity."

"That was the General's funeral. You have to show respect."

"They got no right to sneer at me."

"Eli, I didn't mind that you fought for the bluecoats. I didn't even mind that I missed marching in the parade. But I *did* want to pay my respects to the General."

Boom goes the minute gun.

"It ain't 'bout the General. I liked the General — even if he was mean to you and me."

I snort in indignation. "He never had a bad word for me. He sent *me* on an important mission."

He kicks a stone down the road. "I meant no disrespect to the General. Just to Junior and Lug."

"They did nothing wrong."

He cocks his head and looks at me suspiciously. "You taking their side now?"

"It's not the same. There's a war."

His face turns red. "Oh yeah? Well what about this?" He pulls the pouch I gave him from under his shirt and waves it at me. "What about blood brothers? What about alternate loyalty?"

"What?"

"Alternate loyalty. That's what you said. No one is more important."

"I said *ultimate* loyalty, Eli. And that doesn't mean you can make people angry and expect me to stand up for you."

He turns and stomps toward Prideaux Street.

"I'd do it for you," he calls back.

Oath of Allegiance

October 1812

We hurry past the ruins of the courthouse. It stinks of dead fire. His side did this — his people. He's one of them. As we approach the house, Ginger barks joyfully from the other side of the door, and when Eli opens it, she leaps out to greet us. One look at our faces and she slinks away below the table.

Boom goes the minute gun.

He sits by the window, and I take the stool by the hearth. From beyond the town, the fifes and drums fall silent. The tune has been there all along, but I don't notice it until it's gone. Then, from across the town, a volley of muskets. They're lowering General Brock and Colonel Macdonell into their graves now. I would have been there to honour them, if I didn't have to stand guard over this ingrate. He's retreated back into silence. And so have I.

Boom goes the minute gun.

From below the table, Ginger lifts her ears. She rises to her feet and trots out to the lobby and whines at the front door. Someone opens it and she barks cheerfully. In storms Mina.

"Sakes, you two! I can't take my eyes off you a minute and you get yourselves in big trouble."

I rise from my stool, but Eli just slumps in the chair.

"Little brother, you look at me. Right *now*." But Eli turns his back. "You got no cause to be acting that way," she scolds. She whips off her bonnet and slams it on the table. "You *look* at me, little brother." He droops his head lower.

"He was mad at William and Henry," I offer.

"It don't matter what he was mad at. The whole durned town thinks he insulted the General. And General Brock was a good man."

I signal for Mina to follow me, and we leave the kitchen, cross the lobby into the parlour and close the door. "He saw William and Henry," I say. "That set him off."

Her eyes are sharp with anger, but they soften with surprise.

"How do you know?"

"He told me."

"He's talking?"

"For a little bit. Then we had a fight."

"Fists?"

"Not this time."

She shakes her head. "Well, it's a start." Then she

drills those blue eyes into me again. "He say anything about Pa?"

I shake my head.

"You see him?"

"Who?"

"Pa."

"Where?"

"I thought I caught sight of him at the back of the crowd — staying away from the others."

"He wouldn't be there, Mina. There's no way he would be there."

"But I was nearly sure of it — Pa standing at the back of the crowd, watching you two."

"He can't fight for the other side and then just walk into town. He'd be arrested."

"I could swear that I saw him."

"How'd he get here? Where did he go?"

"I don't know, Jake. I looked at you two, then back, but he was gone."

"He'll be in big trouble if they catch him, Mina. He swore the oath of allegiance, and they'll say he committed treason by fighting against the King."

Mina shrugs. "Ain't no big deal. Eli swore it too."

"What?"

"Lots of folks said they'd be loyal, just to get the authorities off their backs."

"But not Eli — surely not!"

"He didn't tell you?"

Then Ginger barks — barks as furiously as if she's ready to tear someone apart.

"Wait here." I slip into the lobby and peer out the window. Mr. McKenney hobbles up the walkway on his wooden leg. He carries his musket over his shoulder and looks toward the house.

"Mr. Gibson?" he calls. "You in there?"

I open the front door a crack. Ginger scratches at the kitchen door and barks.

"My father's not home, Mr. McKenney."

"The McCabe boy in there?"

I step outside. "He's under our protection, Mr. McKenney."

He rests the stock of his musket on the paving stones. "Not any more. Magistrate Dunwoody wants me to arrest him. Now deliver him over."

"There's no place for you to put him. The jail's burnt down."

"You let me worry about that. Turn him over."

"Do you have a warrant?"

"What?"

"A warrant. For his arrest."

"I don't need a warrant. I do what the magistrate tells me, and if you're smart, you'll do it too."

"You can't just come into people's houses."

"Don't tell me what I can and cannot do, boy. Step aside. And control that dog or I'll shoot it."

"No, sir."

"What?"

"No, sir. You cannot come in."

"Your father will hear about this."

"You have no right to enter this house without a warrant. And you have no right to jail Eli without a charge."

He glares at me with his one good eye. He glances behind me at the door, where Ginger barks and scratches from the other side. "Oh, there's no trouble finding a charge," he snarls as he pivots on his wooden leg. He calls back over his shoulder, "The whole town saw what he did."

He stomps back toward the centre of town, and the door opens behind me. Ginger spills out and chases down the road, barking and yapping, but Mr. McKenney has rounded the corner.

"I've got to go, Jake," says Mina.

"But — "

"I'm in enough trouble as it is. And my little brother just made things worse."

"But we need to talk."

"Then meet me later tonight. Just say where."

"At the lighthouse. It's where I used to meet Eli."

She walks quickly toward town and even with her coat wrapped against the wind, she moves like a summer breeze. I return to the kitchen. Eli watches me from the chair, but the anger is gone from his eyes.

"I know a man with a wooden leg named McKenney," he says.

I'm in no mood for old jokes. "Eli, is it true what Mina said?"

"Depends. What'd she say?"

"You swore the oath of allegiance — along with your father."

"Yeah. Reckon."

"Why didn't you tell me?"

"You had other things on your mind."

"What could be more important?" He doesn't reply. "Eli, what could have possibly been more important? We were blood brothers! We told each other everything. Eli?" I can't tell whether he's mad or sad.

"It was your ma dying, Jake. And your little baby sister. You didn't want to talk to me about no oath of allegiance."

And I remember him that day — the day I've tried so hard to forget; Mother's screams still ringing in my ears and shivering me to my fingertips. The screams had stopped and what remained was the weak cry of little lungs and soon those cries would stop too. I sat in the barn in the dark to get away from it all and I heard Eli's footsteps out in the yard and heard Ginger yip in greeting. Didn't she understand? How could she be happy to see anyone? "Where is he, girl?" Eli asked, and a moment later the door slid open and I squinted at the shaft of light. "Jake! Jake, guess what I done?"

And he saw my face and everything changed.

"So why didn't you tell me later?"

"I was gonna, Jake. I really was. But you were feeling so poorly. And then I thought maybe you'd get vexed if you heard I swore. I'm loyal to you, right? How can I be loyal to King George too?"

"But you did it: you swore allegiance to King George?"

"I didn't cut my hand on it or nothing. It weren't no blood oath."

How could he keep that secret from me? But I've kept secrets from him.

"So, who gave you the oath?"

"The General."

"General Brock? You met with the *General* and you didn't tell me?"

"I was with Pa. It was his idea. I was there to support him, and after Pa swore his oath, the General turns to me and he says, 'What about you, young man?' The way he looked at me, Jake, I would have pulled out my knife and cut my palm right there. But he didn't need that."

My mind is racing. "Were there any other witnesses? Did anyone see you?"

"That colonel feller — the one they buried today."

"Lieutenant Colonel Macdonell?"

"That's the one."

Maybe Eli's secret was buried along with the two

witnesses. It's a terrible thought, but there it is. "Then there's no *living* witness?"

"Not but Pa."

And silence descends. We both look away and finally I turn to Eli. "He'll show up. Your father will be . . . right as roosters."

"I ain't so sure, Jake. Lots of fellers fell off the cliffs. Some even threw themselves over, they was so scared of the Injuns."

"Your father wouldn't."

"Yeah. Reckon."

And we let that thought hang there in the kitchen while we sit in silence. But I feel like I've found my blood brother again.

* * *

Eli and I stand silently in the parlour. Father sits on the settee, back straight, legs together. Beside him, Mr. Willcocks holds the knob of his walking stick with both hands as he rests the point on the floor. I glance to him for some kind of support, but he is as grave as Father.

"Perhaps you would rather I leave you alone," says Mr. Willcocks.

Father shakes his head and addresses Eli. "While under this roof, you will live by our standards of behaviour."

"I didn't mean no disrespect," Eli says.

"And one of the standards is that you remain silent until it is your turn to speak."

"Yes, sir," says Eli.

"Look at me when I talk to you."

"Yes, sir." Eli lifts his chin as if it carries a heavy weight. He meets Father's eyes, glances down, looks up again.

"You disgraced yourself, our family and this house. You've disgraced the entire community."

"I meant no disrespect . . . sir." The sullen tone hangs in the air.

Father pauses. "How could it possibly mean anything *but* disrespect?"

Eli's jaw is tense.

"He means the General, Father. Eli was just reacting to — "

"I'll deal with you in a moment, young man."

"Yes, Father."

"Robert, if I may . . . " Mr. Willcocks raises his hand. "I don't condone what the lad has done. It is an inexcusable breach of decorum. But while we cannot excuse, I think we can understand. The boy seems to have come back to being himself just at the moment he had to confront his two . . . two . . . adversaries."

"He had a sack full of acorns," Father says. He turns to Eli. "You must have gone there with malice aforethought."

"I don't know no Alice, sir. I was there with Jake."

Silence falls on the room. The two men aren't used to how Eli talks — or rather, how he hears things. But I'm not sure what Father's talking about either. Then Mr. Willcocks snickers and suppresses a smile.

"No, Eli," he says. "The word is *malice.* Malice aforethought means you went to the funeral with the intention of doing bad things — like throwing acorns at the mourners."

"But . . . but I didn't. I didn't even know we were going to a funeral."

"How could you not *know*?" Father's voice rises in annoyance. "And why did you bring all those acorns?"

"I . . . I don't know . . . sir. I saw Junior and Lug looking so uppity, and them acorns was just there."

I'd better speak. "He's been gathering them since the battle, Father. It started when we were sitting down on the Heights. He can't stop picking up acorns and putting them in his haversack or his pockets. I don't think he realizes he's doing it."

The clock ticks while Father and Mr. Willcocks consider this. Finally Mr. Willcocks says, "The boy has been suffering from some kind of shock."

"That's no excuse."

"No, Robert, it is not. But it helps explain."

"And how will he *explain* to the rest of the community?"

"I wish I still had my newspaper," Mr. Willcocks says. "We'd publish his apology."

Father turns back to Eli. "*Are* you sorry, Eli?"

"Yes, sir. I meant no disrespect to the General. I meant no dishonour to your family. I'm sorry I did it." He pauses. "I'll make things right," he says.

"And how do you intend to do that?"

"I dunno, sir. Whatever needs to be done. Sweep the streets. Scrub the doorways. Clean out the piss-pots at Government House. Tell me and I'll do it."

Mr. Willcocks lifts his head and says to Father, "A sign of public contrition might be in order, you know."

"I'll help," I add. "Whatever Eli has to do, I'll do too."

Father considers this. "I will have a word with Magistrate Dunwoody, but I don't think you'll be let off that easy. I think you should — "

From beyond the parlour door, Ginger barks as though she's defending our house from invasion — what a ruckus! Then a heavy knock on the outside door — as if someone is pounding it with a stick.

"Jacob, please answer the door."

Mr. McKenney stands in the yard with his wooden leg and his good leg braced to make a stand, a redcoat sergeant and two soldiers behind him. He thrusts out a piece of paper.

"You want a warrant? Here's a warrant. Now turn over the McCabe boy."

Rule of Law

October 1812

The light beam sweeps across the lake. It's so calm out there, with the waves lapping on the beach. Ginger's ears perk forward. Footsteps crunch on the gravel. She leaps to her feet and barks into the night. From across the town, other dogs bark in reply. Every dog in town baying into the night.

Then a female voice calls from below the ridge, "Shhh, girl. It's just me." A shadow climbs through the pathway up from the shore. "If this is your idea of a secret meeting place, Jakie, you best tell Ginger 'bout it." Mina tromps up the beach and grins in the moonlight. "This where you 'n' my brother used to drink Pa's hooch?"

"It was only that one time."

"Uh-huh."

"And besides, I didn't drink any."

She shakes her head and chuckles. "You called this meeting. I hear Pegleg came back to arrest my brother."

"He's at Government House."

"How you know?"

"I followed them. They put him in the room at the end of the hall, upstairs. At the back."

"You talk to him?"

"Not yet. But you and I should go tomorrow."

"Sakes, Jake, they ain't gonna let me talk to him."

"They can't keep *you* away, surely!"

"You think they trust me? Daughter of Cornelius McCabe — the man who wouldn't swear allegiance? Sister of the boy who dropped his pants at the funeral?" She stands in the moonlight, her hands on her hips — not defiant, exactly, but ready to take on anything.

"But don't you want to talk to him?" She gives me a scornful look, as though the question is too stupid to answer. "If Mr. McKenney is his jailor . . . "

An idea begins to form in my mind. Eli and Mr. McKenney once had a kind of partnership: Eli would bring Mr. McKenney his father's homebrew, and Mr. McKenney gave the McCabe tannery the contents of the jail's piss-pots. They used to get along pretty well. How can we take advantage of that?

"We'll be able to visit him some day," I say.

"But not tonight?"

"Mr. McKenney was too angry today. Give him some time to cool down." I think about the look on his face when he came to the door. "Maybe a week or two."

"I can't wait 'til he cools down," says Mina. "I need to talk to my brother now."

"Let's see what we can do." We head down the path toward town, Ginger trotting ahead. The streets are quiet and dark as we walk to the centre of town. A clump of lilac bushes separates the grounds at Government House from the market square. A few leaves cling to the twigs, but the branches provide a bit of cover.

I make a loon call, followed by three owl hoots. The building remains dark. I repeat the signal and up on the second floor, the curtains stir and a window opens.

"Jake?" Eli calls in a low whisper.

"Mina's here too," I reply, loud enough to carry.

"You steady, little brother?" Mina whispers.

"Bed's nice," he says. "Food's good. Hope they don't build no jail any time soon."

"They gonna get you a lawyer?" she asks.

"I don't rightly know."

"We'll get you out of there," I say, although I don't know how.

Mina raises her whisper a little. "What happened to Pa, Eli? When'd you last see him?"

Eli hesitates before he answers. "We was running for the cliffs, but . . . "

"Steady, little brother."

"We was running for our lives."

I glance over my shoulder to the corner of the house.

"Hush," says Mina.

"I *lost* him, sis."

She pauses before she replies, "I saw him. Twice."

"What?" That's me, voice too loud.

"At the funeral parade this morning. Like I told you," she says to me. Then she turns to Eli. "And again this evening. I was upstairs at the Dunwoodys'. I looked out and I just caught sight of him — standing back there in the market square — looking up here. I didn't know it was your window. Reckon *he* did."

"Mina," I interrupt, "he *can't* be here."

"I'm telling you what I saw. I ran out to find him, but he was gone."

"How was he dressed, sis? His uniform?"

"I never seen him in his uniform. He was wearing his coat."

"He's gonna get himself arrested."

Mina chuckles. "That's one way to keep track of you both."

"This is crazy, you two. There's no way he can be here."

"Jake, I'm just telling you what I saw. He'll show up again. I'm sure of it."

Eli says, "They say I gotta stand trial, Jake. Some muckety-muck is coming from York and he's gonna prosci . . . prosti . . . Put me on trial."

"Prosecute?"

"That's right."

"For showing your bum?" asks Mina.

"Reckon."

"It's such a skinny bum," she says. "Ain't worth going to trial for that."

"What's some muckety-muck from York got to do with me anyway?" Then he goes quiet and the curtains close.

We wait. When nothing happens, I nod and we slip away down the road toward the lake.

"What we gonna do, Jake?"

"We'll get him out."

"How? Attack Government House? Just the two of us?"

I think about this before replying.

"We'll have to use the rule of law."

"You setting to be a lawyer, Jakie?"

The idea of defending Eli in a court of law seems about as far-fetched as attacking Government House with a sixteen-year-old girl. "Mina, we'll do whatever it takes."

* * *

I stare up at the ceiling in the dark. I don't close my eyes because of what might appear. Sometimes I see Good Spirit with his chest shot away and the white bone poking from the gore. Sometimes a horse lies in a field of pumpkins, with its head blown to bits. Sometimes a bateau swirls in the dark river with a man looking at me with dead eyes. Sometimes a cannonball rips into a soldier as he stands over the body of General Brock. Sometimes a crow hops onto the face of a man who has been scalped. If I keep my eyes closed, the scalped man turns into Eli, and Mountain Lion has ripped away his hair.

I used to want to be a soldier, but I don't want ever to see war again. If a soldier could spring Eli free, though, I'd be one for him. But this is no job for a soldier. It's a job for the rule of law — and a free press. That's what Mr. Willcocks would say. I need to learn more. I need to find out what they plan to do with Eli and how it can be stopped. I need to study the law.

* * *

"I say, is that *Blackstone* you have there?"

I look up from my reading. The fellow standing at the other end of the table is scarcely taller than I am, but he holds his pointed chin high and he seems to be looking down his long, thin nose at me. I lift the book up to show him the spine.

He arches one eyebrow. "Will you be long with it?" His voice is flat and calm, and his blue eyes study me. "I'm afraid I'm in a bit of a hurry."

I remove the sheets of paper where I've been

making my notes, close the tome and push it along the table toward him. "I can look at it later."

He gives a thin-lipped smile. "Awfully kind of you." He removes his overcoat, sets it on a chair, takes the seat across the table and leans forward as if to get a closer look. When he's sitting down, he doesn't appear short any more. He is a young man — not much older than William and Henry.

He picks up the book and opens it at random. "This is the only copy of *Blackstone* in this town. Still" — he turns those cold, blue eyes back on me — "we should be thankful the library wasn't burned to the ground." He runs his hands over the leather, then frowns at me. "You're rather young to be spending your afternoons in the company of Lord Blackstone."

"I'm doing it for a friend," I tell him.

His eyes look bemused — a tiny flicker of warmth. "Greater love hath no man than this, that he should spend an afternoon poring over English jurisprudence." He rises from his chair and has to lean forward a long way to offer his hand. "My name is Robinson. How do you do." Our hands barely reach across the big table.

"Gibson," I reply. "Jacob."

"Well, young Gibson, do you want to become a lawyer?" He takes his seat again and folds his arms as he looks across at me.

"I . . . I never thought of it."

"With whom do you study now?"

"Dominie Burns — "

But before I can finish, the door behind him swings open, and a gust of October wind rustles the paper on the table. He leans back in his chair and stretches his neck to see who is coming.

"Hello, gentlemen," he calls out. "I can't escape you for an afternoon, it seems."

From beyond the door, a familiar voice replies, "You're too easy to find, Bev."

A second voice adds, "Look for the law books, and there you'll find Robinson."

I know who they are before they step in and close the door.

"Gibson!" says William. "You're keeping better company these days."

"Ah!" Mr. Robinson looks at me. "You know one another already, of course."

Henry stands at the end of the table. The new fellow sits like a prince, with a huge bodyguard beside him. "We've told you about Gibson," Henry says.

Uh-oh. What have they been saying? My friendship with Eli? My old job at Mr. Willcocks's newspaper? The fight at the bridge last election day? What have they told him about the acorn fight and the funeral procession?

Well, I could tell Mr. Robinson a thing or two

about William Dunwoody and Henry Ecker. I wonder what these law books say about breaking in to someone's premises to destroy a printing press, or burning down someone's tannery business.

William says, "He's the one who fought alongside Norton."

"Really!" Mr. Robinson rises to his feet. "This is the young hero?"

"Held the line with the Mohawk until General Sheaffe arrived," says Henry.

"Well, young Gibson, let me shake your hand." Once more we stretch across the broad expanse of table. "Splendid work. Your father fought with Colonel Butler in the late rebellion, I understand. I should like to meet him sometime."

I mumble, "I'm sure he'd be pleased to . . . "

William sidles up beside Mr. Robinson. "Play your cards right," he says, "and you'll be invited to the wedding lunch."

"Ah yes! The lovely widow Lovelace," says Mr. Robinson. "My, it's a small world, isn't it? Charming woman."

"Shall I let her know you'd like an invitation?" asks William.

"You, Dunwoody? I should think that young Gibson here will make the arrangements." He turns his attention back to me. "That would be splendid, Gibson. I should try to get to know society while

I'm here." He rises in his place and puts on his overcoat. He lifts Lord Blackstone's heavy volume and follows Henry out the door. Is he allowed to take books away? Who would ever try to stop him? William stays behind, looking at me for a long time.

"You have an opportunity, Jacob — a clean slate. You're a hero. I know you were with McCabe at the funeral procession. I trust that you had nothing to do with his behaviour. Make your choices wisely." He turns and leaves without waiting for my reply.

* * *

They say I'm a hero.

"Jacob?"

I don't want to be a hero.

"Jacob . . . "

I just want things to be like they were before.

"Jacob, will you answer the question, please?"

"He's off to dreamland again, Papa."

I glare at George. She has the place beside Father. Abby sits across from me. And at the other end of the table, facing Father, Mrs. Lovelace has taken *my* chair.

"Uh . . . Yes, Father?"

Four pairs of eyes, all looking at me.

"Is there anyone you want to invite to the wedding luncheon?"

George's fork is raised halfway to her mouth as she

waits, gaping. Her mother nods at her sternly, and she puts the food down again. I study my carrots and beets. This would be the time to talk about that Robinson fellow I met this afternoon, but there are more important matters. Do I dare ask for Eli to be released so he can attend? Maybe I can invite two guests.

I look up at Father. "Can we invite Mina?"

Father studies me a moment, then looks down the table at Mrs. Lovelace. The mantle clock ticks.

"That's the *McCabe* girl," says George.

"I've met her," says Abby. "She's nice."

"But isn't she in *service*?" says George.

I glower. "She works for the Dunwoody family."

"We wouldn't want to make her feel uncomfortable, dear," says Mrs. Lovelace sweetly. "After all, the Dunwoodys will be there, and she might feel awkward socializing with her betters."

I don't dare look at Mrs. Lovelace. I will not let her see my anger.

"Jacob's turning red," chirps George.

"I would like Mina to come." I grit my teeth. "As my guest."

Father watches me calmly. "I think that can be arranged," he says.

Mrs. Lovelace has a smile as cold as porcelain. That did not go well. I'll ask about inviting Eli when Father and I are alone.

"There's someone else I would like to come,"

Mrs. Lovelace begins. "The new attorney general is in town for a visit. We might prevail upon him to return for the wedding luncheon. It would serve us well to send him an invitation."

The attorney general! That's the "muckety-muck" that Eli was talking about.

"They've replaced poor Macdonell?" asks Father. "So soon?"

"You haven't heard?" says Mrs. Lovelace.

"He's very young," says Abby.

"And handsome," adds George.

"How would you know?" Abby retorts.

"Mama and I saw him coming out of Government House. When we were having tea with Mrs. Dunwoody."

"Yes, he's young, dear," Mrs. Lovelace says.

"Macdonell was young," says Father. "May he rest in peace."

"The new attorney general's even younger," Mrs. Lovelace leans forward conspiratorially. "A protegé of the Reverend Dr. Strachan." She lifts her chin higher. "I was thinking that Jacob might benefit from Dr. Strachan's instruction."

"Send him to York for school?" asks Father.

"Certainly he would receive a superior education."

Father ponders this. "It would be safer — farther from the border. But maybe all of you should go to York."

"We're just getting established here, dear. Perhaps later."

"But Jacob can't leave us," says Abby.

Her mother interjects, "I understand that the Dunwoody boy is to be sent to York as well."

"But Jacob's going to be our brother," says Abby.

"Henry Ecker's going to York too," says George, the know-it-all.

Abby ignores her. "And we're all just getting acquainted."

Mrs. Lovelace raises her voice to brook no contradiction. "Jacob would meet the best in society from across the province."

"I couldn't go," I say. "I've got to help Eli."

"Don't you think it would be wise," says Mrs. Lovelace, as calmly as the lake at dawn, "to distance yourself from that boy?"

"He's my *friend*."

"Yes, dear," she says, "and loyalty is a great virtue. But there are times when one must choose one's friends more carefully."

A Prisoner Visit

October 1812

"You realize, you young people, that I'm taking a big risk here." Mr. McKenney draws on the jug and his Adam's apple bobs while he swallows. "A mighty big risk." He lost part of his jaw at the Battle of Saratoga, and liquid dribbles from the corner of his mouth. He wipes it away with his sleeve and lands the jug with a *thud* beside the chessboard. "Still" — he smacks his lips — "I'm happy to have the refreshment. And the company, on this night of all nights."

"Me and Jake, we're much obliged," says Mina. "And my little brother too. Ain't that right, little brother?"

On the edge of his bed, Eli beams. After two weeks, he's been allowed visitors — or rather, we have contrived a way to see him. Mina has brought a jug of homebrew — just like Eli used to. Whisky is plentiful and cheap in our town, but Mr. McCabe's product was well-respected and much sought-after and, according to Mr. McKenney, this batch is almost as good.

Now that we're in the room with Eli, it's much easier to talk, but there's not a lot we can say with Mr. McKenney right here.

A wallpapered room in Government House makes a comfortable jail cell and sure beats anything Eli would have had before the courthouse burned down. He's probably never slept on a better bed, and a washstand and bowl are luxuries he never had at home. There's even a small table for the chessboard. The only sign that the room has been refitted for a new purpose is the iron grate newly installed on the window. There's a trap door in the ceiling. Where does that go?

"You won't be having some for yourself? Something to keep the goblins away?" Mr. McKenney offers the jug to the three of us in turn.

"We brought it for you," says Mina. "And we're much obliged."

"The lads have all gone. There's revelry at the fort tonight, you'll understand. But they've left me alone with young McCabe in a haunted place on All Hallows' Eve."

"Don't get him started with his ghost stories," warns Eli.

"But Government House can't be haunted, Mr. McKenney," I offer. "It's not old enough."

He shakes his head. "People were living here for thousands of years before some army engineer cast his eye on this spot and said, 'We'll put headquarters right there.' I tell you, something must have happened in the long ago at this very place. I can feel it."

"I'm not listening," says Eli.

I don't want to hear anything about ghosts either, but Mr. McKenney has the bit between his teeth.

"And I *hear* things," he says. "In the middle of the night."

"What kind of things?" asks Mina.

"*Don't* get him started," says Eli.

"Miss, I won't be tempting the wee folk by talking about such things — not on the night when the portals between our world and theirs open wide."

This is getting bad — really bad. I don't dare glance at the window. This is not why we came here. How are we possibly going to talk to Eli?

"I like this night," says Mina. "You can tell fortunes tonight."

Mr. McKenney tilts his head to look at her. "Is that a fact?"

"Where Eli and me come from, this is the night a girl can predict who she's gonna marry, but you need an apple."

"Just an apple?" asks the jailer.

"Some girls use molten lead, but Ma taught me to use an apple peel."

I see what Mina is trying to do. "Can you get us one of those?" I ask.

"Not an apple *peel*," says Mina. "An apple."

Mr. McKenney looks at me doubtfully. "You want me to go down to the cellar? In the dark? On this night?"

"You'd take a candle, of course," says Mina. "Why not get four apples? One for each of us. I'll tell you your future bride, Mr. McKenney."

He laughs nervously. "Now, don't be getting the hopes up of a tired old soldier with but one leg and one eye."

"Didn't you know, sir? There's someone for everyone." Did she actually just wink at him?

"Maybe one of you young people can go fetch the apples from the cellar."

"You'd let one of us wander through Government House?" I ask.

"Maybe someone should come with me."

"I'm sure we shouldn't be down there," I say.

"We don't want you to be getting into trouble, Mr. McKenney," says Mina. "No one's ever gonna know if we just stay right here."

Mr. McKenney considers. "I'll have to lock you up in here while I'm gone. Nothing personal."

"Of course," I reply.

"Just so we understand one another." He takes a candle holder from the sill. Shadows dance across the walls as he hobbles to the door, *step-THUMP, step-THUMP.* His light shrinks down the hallway.

As soon as he's far enough away, Mina whispers, "Jakie's been studying the law, little brother."

"What're they gonna do to me?"

"They'll try you at the next quarter session," I reply. I stop and we all listen as the *step-THUMP* of the wooden leg pounds up the hallway, accompanied by the jangle of keys.

"I won't be but a moment," Mr. McKenney says as he swings the door closed. A key rattles in the escutcheon, and the bolt slides into place before the *step-THUMP, step-THUMP* moves back down the hallway.

Mina and I join Eli on the bed where we can talk in low voices. "Magistrate Dunwoody's probably going to try the case," I say. *Step-thump.*

"Not some muckety-muck from York?" Eli doesn't seem to be bothered by the sound of Mr. McKenney's leg pounding about — he must be used to it. But I hesitate before I answer.

"It's only a misdemeanour, Eli." *Step-thump, step-thump.* Don't think about it! "You only need a justice of the peace."

He frowns. "I'd be better off with the muckety-muck. So what's the worst that can happen?"

"Jake?" says Mina. "You aright?"

"Sorry." I can no longer hear the step of the good leg, only the *thump* of the wooden peg. "It's all based on precedent."

"What's Mr. Madison got to do with it?" Eli raises his voice in indignation and Mina hushes him.

"Sakes," she whispers. "Folks hereabouts think he started the war."

I pull myself together. "Not president. *Precedent*. It means what was decided before — in similar cases."

Mina asks, "Someone show their *bum* at a funeral before?"

Thump . . . Thump. It's only Mr. McKenney and it's far away, but the sound spreads in my imagination like pox.

"You *sure* you're aright?"

Only one way to fight it: get back to the matter we came here for. "In 1790, there was a man who walked naked into a room," I whisper quickly. "He started shouting that he was a rebel and that he supported the United States. When he — "

Step-thump at the bottom of the stairs stops me in mid-sentence. Mina's face looks worried, but whether it's because of the sound or because we're running out of time, I can't tell.

"That ain't the same," Eli says. "What's the matter with you two?"

I put on a brave face, even though my heart pounds louder than the *step-THUMP* that rises from the stairwell. "It's the closest precedent I can find." I look up at the trap door in the ceiling. What's behind there, anyway? What if it started to open?

"Slim, you been studying real hard."

Step-THUMP, step-THUMP coming up the stairs.

"Get back to your chairs," Eli hisses. Mina and I look at each other and scurry back to our places as the key rattles in the lock. What if it's *not* Mr. McKenney? What if, on the other side of that door, a spirit from the battlefield treads those boards? *Step-THUMP.*

But the door opens and it's only the jailer — four plump apples tucked under his arm. "Not a night for poking about in cellars," he sighs. "Even the dormouse gave me a fright down there." He places the candle on the washstand, and the room brightens. "One thing about this country," he says, "the apples are excellent."

"Put them on the table," says Mina. "Close your eyes and choose one." We each pick an apple. I squeeze mine hard. "Now take your knife," she says.

"What knife?" asks Mr. McKenney.

"You have a knife with you. Right?"

His face falls. "Not with me, no."

Step-THUMP. Step-THUMP.

When we gather again on Eli's bed, I'm no longer sure whether it's to whisper together, or to gather courage from one another in the face of that eerie sound.

"Sakes, brother, this is some scary place," says Mina.

"You feel it too?" he says. "Sometimes I can't sleep after Pegleg's told me stories."

"But what about now? What about that noise?"

"What noise?" says Eli. And it's as if he hears the pounding for the first time. His face goes pale.

"What's behind that trap door?" I ask.

"The attic. Nothing up there but spiders." He shivers in disgust. "I hate spiders."

"You've been up there?"

"Reckon. There's an awful lot of spiders."

"Just hope that there sound doesn't start coming from the attic," says Mina.

"Don't *say* that!" says Eli and he glances at the trap door, truly alarmed. We sit there for a moment, listening.

"What would happen" — I whisper — "if the noises came back, but it *wasn't* Mr. McKenney?"

"Slim, don't you get started. McKenney's bad enough with his wee folk and banshees. Come on now, just tell me what they done to that feller what was naked."

"He was thrown out of the country."

"That ain't so bad," says Mina.

"That's all I want," adds Eli. "Ain't it?" He doesn't take his eye off the attic door.

Step-thump up the stairway. *Step-THUMP* up the hallway.

Eli's eyes meet mine. Do I look that scared? But he

pulls himself together and says, "Slim, you're the best friend a feller could ever have."

Step-THUMP. The key rattles in the door, and none of us says a word as the hinges squeak open. Mr. McKenney looks like he's as glad to see us as we are to see it's only him.

He passes around the paring knife, and each of us takes a turn with our apple and tossing the peel over our shoulder. Mina studies how it lands and the shape it makes.

Eli's is stretched out but curled up at either end. Mina pronounces it to be a canoe, and I can see how it might look that way if you use your imagination. We discuss what this might possibly mean and agree that perhaps he will marry someone far away — maybe in the fur trade country. Mr. McKenney's apple peel lands neatly in a near-perfect spiral. He says the shape represents a zero and proves he has no prospects. But Mina disagrees, offering that it means he will marry a portly woman, or perhaps a woman already with child. Mina declares that my apple peel represents a grand house and that I will surely marry into wealth — or, at least, someone associated with a mansion.

And Mina's apple peel? It falls into the shape of a wavy line. Eli protests that it forms the letter *W* and that he would rather go to the gallows than see his sister marry William Dunwoody.

But she says, "I don't think that there peel's a double-u, little brother. I think those are scales of justice. I'm gonna marry a lawyer — or maybe a judge." She glances up at me and I look away. Neither of us mentions it again when I walk her home, but I try to think about it as I fall to sleep, so I can forget the awful feeling as we listened to *step-THUMP* in the night. It was our imaginations at work, I tell myself — only the power of our imaginations.

* * *

I am fishing near the bulrushes below the piers, with Navy Hall behind me and the American fort downstream. Gulls hover above, catching the wind and staying in place as if each was fastened to a kite string. They stare at me with beady eyes and open their mouths to call, but they make no sound. I fasten a minnow to a hook and cast it into the river.

And there! I've caught a fish — maybe the biggest muskie in Lake Ontario. I bend my legs and arch my back to haul it in, but it doesn't fight — it's just a dead weight. Maybe I've caught only a log.

Upriver, blue shapes float on the surface — drowned soldiers carried from the Queenston cliffs. I pull my catch to the shore and my hook is embedded in the uniform of a big man. He lies face down in the water, but I recognize him by his cannonball shape — Eli's father, bloated even bigger by his journey through the water.

I want to run. I want to wake up. But the gulls swirl around me. They are not connected by kite strings any more; they swoop and cackle. With both hands I roll Eli's pa onto his back. His skin is pale as lake foam. His head tilts, and a big eel emerges from his mouth and slithers into the river. The gulls swoop in and begin to rip through the tattered uniform.

One gull turns and cocks its head to look at me. "This ain't Pa," it says in Eli's voice. "Pa ain't here no more."

And that's when I bolt up in bed. I don't dare look at the window.

The King's Justice

November 1812

"Father?"

"Yes, Jacob."

"I think that's Eli over there."

Father straightens his back and winces. He's getting too old for this kind of work. The sun hangs low in the east, and he shades his eyes as he squints to where Captain Runchey's militia clears away the burnt timber and other debris. These men live with their families at the edge of town and they've been put together in one unit. The British army has also sent a company of redcoats from Fort George. Civilians, militia and redcoats, together we clean up our shattered courthouse, our faces and clothes caked with the same grey of dust and ash. But I can tell it's Eli. Where everyone else moves slowly, methodically, Eli plays, even hauling burnt timbers.

"Can I join him?"

"Help me with this first," Father grunts as we lift what was once part of the roof. We carry it over the wreckage to the road.

"One, two, three, drop."

It lands hard on the frosted ground. I look at Father.

"Go ahead," he says. "I'll rest a minute."

Ginger and I leave him sitting on the pile of half-burnt wood and we scramble over the stones and shattered planks. When Ginger realizes who that is at the other end of the wreckage, she yips and scampers across to Eli.

"Slim! Give us a hand here."

"They let you out!"

"Yeah!" He smiles and his teeth are bright against the dust and grime on his face. I lend a hand as Runchey's men bring down the old jail door and carry it to a wagon. Eli nods for me to follow and we take up shovels and pile dirt and broken wood into a wheelbarrow. We each take a handle and roll toward King Street.

"You still playing chess with Mr. McKenney all day?"

"Betcha I could beat-cha now."

"Not likely."

"I'll show you. I'm even beating Mr. McKenney."

At the foot of King Street, we pass Eli's old house and his father's tannery and we dump the dirt near the water. The ice will pile up here this winter, and when it sweeps out in the spring thaw, there will be no sign that there was ever a heap of debris that was once the seat of justice in Lincoln County.

"I had a dream the other night — after we visited you. A real bad one."

"Corn, Slim. I got to say, I was really spooked that night."

"You weren't scared of the noise at first."

He shrugs. "Not 'til I saw how scared it made you and sis. And *you* brought up them spiders."

"I asked about the trap door in the ceiling — that's all."

"Reckon we're all scared of something. I ain't surprised you had nightmares."

"The dream was about your father."

He studies the fort that rises like a castle across the river. "I don't reckon we'll see Pa again," he says softly.

"No." I put my hand on his shoulder. "I don't think so."

"Mina says she keeps seeing him."

I look at the pebbles at my feet.

Eli sighs. "So close, ain't it?" He's looking across at the stars and stripes flying above Fort Niagara.

I take a deep breath and say, "It's just a short boat ride."

He considers that for a long moment. "Yeah. Reckon."

"We could make a sprint for it now. Find a boat. Get you across the border."

He crinkles his nose. "I thought you was gonna be my lawyer."

"They'll send you there anyway. We'd just be saving some time."

"I gave 'em my word not to escape — not while I'm on this here work detail." He starts heading up the hill with the wheelbarrow. "Way I figure it, Junior's pa'll give me a tongue-lashing, then they'll boot me out of the Canadas and that'll be that."

He may be right — but since the dream the other night, I've got a bad feeling about this. "What would it take to break you out?"

"Leave the best bed I ever had?"

"There's the trap door."

He shudders in disgust. "I *hate* spiders."

"But no windows up in the attic? No other trap door?"

"Nothing, Slim. Just spiders."

"What if we got you an axe or something to cut through the roof?"

"Yeah. But I'd make too much noise."

"What about a file to cut the bars?"

His eyes brighten. "That might work."

"How long do you think it would take?" I ask.

"A few days."

"They'd discover what you're doing."

"Yeah. Reckon. Might as well just go through with the trial, Slim."

As we reach the top of the hill, a group of men comes down the road from Government House — officers in red coats and civilians in top hats. They gather at the corner across from the library.

Eli doesn't seem to notice them. "If I was to make a break . . . The way I see it, Jake, the best way would be to get Mr. McKenney's keys and unlock the door."

"Where does he keep them?" I try to remember the details of the other night. It took Mr. McKenney a while to lock the three of us in.

"On a hook by the stairs. But no way they're gonna let you get to them."

"Maybe Father would help."

"Reckon?"

I look across the debris of the courthouse. Father is still sitting there. He really is too old for this kind of work.

"Let's think about it," I say. "Talk to you later."

"I ain't going far."

I watch Eli join Captain Runchey's detail, then cross over to Father. He looks so tired.

"Maybe you should go home," I suggest.

"Let's finish this first."

As we carry another burnt log to the side of the road, I watch the group gathered at the street corner. The red uniforms are so bright against the ashes and dust. A soldier in a cocked hat holds out a map in both hands while he talks. After we've cleared the rubble, they will build the new courthouse and jail, but in this man's imagination, it already stands. He talks to an officer with gold epaulettes and a feathered hat.

"One, two, three, drop."

"Father, that's General Sheaffe, isn't it?"

Before he can answer, a voice pipes up from the group, "I say! Gibson, is that you?"

The young man I met the other day, Robinson, picks his way over the debris in buckled shoes. Father and I lean on our shovels as we wait. "Look at the two of you! You could pass as some of Runchey's men." He smiles.

He looks so clean and well-groomed among all this destruction, not a speck of ash on him. How do I address him? Robinson? Mr. Robinson? William and Henry call him Bev.

"Hello." I hesitate. "I'd like you to meet my father."

"The hero from the last war! Well, sir, I should like to shake your hand." He looks at Father's clothes, covered with ash dust. "Well, perhaps later, then." He gives a little bow. "By the way, I certainly look forward to your pending nuptials, for which invitation I understand I have Gibson junior to thank."

"I beg your pardon?" asks Father.

But Mr. Robinson turns back to me. "Thank you for your intercession. It looks as though I shall have to return frequently to Newark, but never for so pleasant an occasion as your father's wedding to the lovely Mrs. Lovelace."

"You're Robinson?" asks Father. "You're the new attorney general?"

"Only on an acting basis at present, but yes, for my sins. Sorry. How *gauche* of me not to introduce myself." And then he stops chattering. Stops cold as he stares past Father to Runchey's militia at work at the far end.

"Is there something wrong, Mr. Robinson?" Father asks.

"Is that the McCabe boy over there, working with the others?"

"Eli?" I reply. "He's sorry about the funeral. He wants to do something for the community."

"This won't do," mutters Robinson. "Won't do at all."

"He's given his parole," I offer.

"His *parole*? I wouldn't take that rascal's word on anything."

"Eli's a good lad," says Father. "A bit rough around the edges — "

"Mr. Gibson, that young rapscallion swore an oath to protect His Majesty. And last month he was apprehended taking up arms against the King. Oh, we'll make a lesson of him."

"Mr. Robinson, he's just a boy, too young to pledge — "

"Mr. Gibson, I know for a fact that he did sign the oath."

"How?" I blurt. "Nobody knows."

Mr. Robinson gives me a long, careful stare. "Can

you provide Crown evidence, Jacob?" I say nothing and he turns back to Father. "Mr. Gibson, the McCabe boy signed a document. Signed it with his own hand — which is more than McCabe *père* was able to accomplish. Maybe he took that oath lightly and did not consider the consequences. But I assure you, sir, that we do *not* take it lightly. And believe me: there will be consequences."

"What will you do?"

"Why, put him on trial, of course. And trust in a verdict of guilty."

"But this is serious," Father says.

"Treason? Oh, indeed. A hanging offence. Now, if you'll excuse me."

As he returns to his group, he calls to a lieutenant who then leads a sergeant and two soldiers across the debris. I can get there first by cutting across, but Father grabs my shoulder and shakes his head sternly.

"But we have to warn Eli . . . "

He doesn't let go of my shoulder — just keeps staring across the lot, his face anxious and puzzled. Ginger watches too. The soldiers seize Eli so suddenly, his head snaps back in surprise, and that's when Ginger barks and sprints across the shattered timbers.

"Ginger! Stop!" I shout. "Come!"

But she won't listen. I shake off Father's hand and chase after her. He calls me, but I pay no attention.

The militia stand in a circle around the soldier who ties Eli's hands behind his back with a leather cord. The sergeant and the other soldier turn to fend off Ginger's attack.

"Stop! Stop! Ginger, *come!*"

She barks and snaps. A soldier swipes at her with the butt of his musket, but she ducks and swerves away. Runchey's men cheer. A soldier raises his musket to shoot, but there are too many people around for a clear aim. She feints in, ducks back out. She gets almost close enough to nip the leg of the soldier who tied Eli's hands, but runs back out again as a bayonet stabs down. The militia cheer again. I break through their circle and swoop down to scoop Ginger up.

She bites me in the cheek. I don't feel it as pain in my skin, more like a pain in my heart, as she growls and snarls and squirms. But I don't let go. No, I won't let go. And now she recognizes me. She stops trying to break free, but she won't stop barking.

"Take that animal and shoot it," instructs the sergeant.

"That will be enough," says the lieutenant. "Boy, control that dog or I'll shoot it myself."

The soldier pushes Eli and he staggers up the road. Captain Runchey's men part to let them pass. Eli looks at me and at Ginger with such bewilderment as they march him up King Street toward Government House.

* * *

"We *can't* let them hang Eli."

"They haven't found him guilty yet."

Father wipes blood off my cheek with his handkerchief. Ginger rests with her nose on her paws, ears down, tail forlorn on the ground. It wasn't her fault. Will I have a scar on my cheek the rest of my life?

"We have to break him out of jail."

Father studies the blood on his handkerchief and looks again at my cheek before dabbing again. "Now how would you do that?"

Should I tell him about the keys? Not yet. "We'll find a way."

Father shakes his head. He sits down slowly on the timbers. "Jacob, that would be unjust."

"What?"

Ginger lifts her head at the tone of my voice. Her eyes look so sad.

Father says, "We have to let due process prevail."

"But Eli's done nothing wrong."

"That's for the courts and the King's justice to decide."

"The King's not here. It's Mr. Robinson and Magistrate Dunwoody."

He takes so much time to answer, as if he needs to gather his strength for each sentence. "There will be a judge and a jury of Eli's peers."

"Will there be any Americans on this jury?"

"Not likely."

"Any boys our age?"

"No."

"Then how can they be his peers?"

He twists his head to stretch his neck and he's making a funny face as he rubs his shoulder, and while he's doing all that, he says, "The jury . . . will be chosen at random among . . . the people who can vote."

"Magistrate Dunwoody didn't let Eli's father vote."

"Yes, I remember." He takes a deep breath.

I pace back and forth, back and forth. "Then maybe he'll try to cheat again."

"Jacob, we count on the trial being fair. This is the King's justice."

"But what if they're wrong? What if they find Eli guilty?"

"He'll have to face" — he pauses for breath — "the consequences."

"You want to see him *hang*?"

"Of *course* not."

"What if it were *me* in jail? What if *I* were to hang?" Is he studying my face? He's not meeting my eyes, exactly, so I pursue the argument. "You've got to help him escape. If they're going to hang him. Right?"

He takes a deep breath and seems to draw his

energy together. "Jacob, I have spent my life defending my King. I have lived my life under the King's justice. I must conduct my life according to the King's laws."

"No! That can't be right. It's not *fair.*"

He looks at me with his sad eyes. He breathes heavily, but has no strength to rise again — nor strength to reply.

"It's not fair and it's not *right.*" I stamp off toward Prideaux Street. Ginger hesitates, then follows beside me, looking up anxiously. She whimpers, looks back and trots in the other direction. What's the matter?

Father no longer sits. He has fallen over and lies on the ground. I sprint back as fast as I can. Some of Captain Runchey's men reach him before I do.

No Escape

November 1812

This is a beautiful church. Mrs. Lovelace and the girls seem to find comfort in this service, these words. Their voices rise high and clear.

Lord, hear our prayer.

In this church, you kneel on little benches to pray. I lean forward enough to see Abby and George on the other side of Mrs. Lovelace. Father is not yet strong enough to kneel, so he sits with the blanket over his knees. When it's time to sing, Mrs. Lovelace and I each take an elbow to support him to his feet. She squeezes his hand. She's probably lonely — he's been lonely too, I guess.

"You must not upset your father," she told me. "Dr. Kerr says he will recover, but he cannot take any excitement. I'm sure you understand, Jacob."

"Yes, Ma'am," I replied.

"You can call me *Mother*, you know."

"Yes, Ma'am."

Lord, hear our prayer.

She was right: he is recovering. But no more work details for him. She also wants him to give up the Lincoln County militia, but he has not agreed to that. He hopes for full recovery. Dr. Kerr is not so sure. But I must help Father get better. I will not upset him again, ever. I promise. Please, God, if only You will make him well again, I will follow in Father's path, his example, his advice.

Lord, hear our prayer.

But how am I going to explain this to Eli?

* * *

Fog rolls in from the lake so thick that I can't see across the field to the tent where the food and drink await. The rubble has been cleared, and now it's time to build. The official party stands like silhouettes cut from black paper and pasted on a grey page. Some silhouettes have military hats; others have top hats. One silhouette sits in a chair — Father, bundled up against the fog. Mrs. Lovelace says it's a great honour for him to join the official party — and she should know. She arranged it.

One of the silhouettes is General Sheaffe, who gives a speech in a low, growly voice that's hard to hear, but everyone applauds politely. Then Mr. Robinson's tenor cuts through the fog. "The enemy tried to strike us down," he says, "but we prevailed. We will build again and affirm our British heritage and our respect for His Majesty and for the rule of law." The audience claps loudly. George jumps up and down, and Mrs. Lovelace places a calming hand on her shoulder.

The speeches finished, Father rises from his chair and takes his place between Mr. Willcocks and Magistrate Dunwoody. The General nods to a captain, the captain nods to a sergeant, who nods to a soldier, who snaps the leads and two horses strain forward. Ropes groan, a pulley squeaks and slowly — oh, so slowly at first — the peak of the wooden frame lifts from the dirt. When it stands perpendicular, the cedar logs slide into the postholes with a satisfying *thud.* Two redcoats step forward, each straining under the weight of a rock the size of a wild turkey. They drop the rocks into the postholes with a knock of stone against wood. Each member of the official party tosses smaller rocks — the size of chickens, of robins, of sparrows. The stone Father deposits is the size of a goose egg and it lands last, a final clatter. The crowd applauds, and soldiers pour liquid cement into the holes. Nothing's going to budge those posts for a hundred years! Then we turn back to the tent to get out of the mist and fill our bellies.

"Gibson," calls a voice. "Glad to see your father looking better." William Dunwoody removes kid gloves from his hands. He looks at me more closely. "What happened to your cheek?"

"I cut it on a nail. In the barn."

"Looks nasty."

"It will heal."

"Ha! Tell the girls it's a duelling scar." He joins me in the flow of people moving toward the tent. "By the way, will the wedding be delayed?"

"They're going ahead."

"Capital. Your future stepmother is a force of nature — nothing will stop her. I do hope we'll see much more of her — and you, of course. Ah, listen to that." William holds up his hand. Hammers pound against nails and the sound echoes in the fog. "They're wasting no time."

"If it was up to me" — Henry Ecker joins us — "we'd build the jail first. Or the gallows."

"All in good time, Henry. It won't take long."

"At least they're building a bigger jail," says Henry. "We're going to need it."

"We'll arrest each and every Yankee-lover in Lincoln County," adds William.

"There's a lot of them," says Henry. "Starting with Turd Boy. Heavens, Gibson, what happened to your face? Sword fight over some lady's honour?"

"Not unless you count the Gibson cow," laughs William. "He ran into a barn nail."

Henry studies my wound more carefully. "Hope you have a poultice. My father makes them from roots. He learned how to do it from the Iroquois."

"Yes," I murmur. "My father makes it."

"That's right. I keep forgetting. Our fathers knew each other — back in the last war."

"We really must have you over to the house," says William. "When your father's feeling better."

We've reached the serving table, and the fork looks small in Henry's hand as he shovels slices of ham and sausage onto his plate. He fills a punch cup and offers it to me.

"You partaking, Gibson?"

"Does it have rum in it?"

"I'm counting on it," he chuckles.

"No, thank you."

"Suit yourself."

"Look, there's Bev," says William. "And there's Mrs. Lovelace with your father. Let's join them."

"In a moment," I reply. But as soon as I've filled my plate, I pour a glass full of punch, and Ginger and I push our way in the opposite direction. Soon the tent has disappeared in the fog behind us.

I'm not looking forward to this, but it has to be done and best to do it with offerings of food and drink.

* * *

"You're a good lad, Jacob Gibson. I've always said that. Haven't I, young McCabe?"

"I wish I could have brought more."

Mr. McKenney drains the glass of rum punch in one long gulp, and liquid trickles down his whiskers as he smacks his lips with a satisfied sigh. Eli sits on the bed and picks at the sausages and ham. Usually he digs into food as if he's not sure whether he will ever eat again, but not today. He's pale and distracted and he stares as if he's listening to something the rest of us can't hear — not just the distant pounding of the hammers.

"They've quite a crew building my new jail," says Mr. McKenney. "They'll have it finished before the snow flies — the walls and roof anyway. Won't be enjoying General Sheaffe's hospitality for much longer, will we, young McCabe?" Mr. McKenney shakes his head and Eli just studies the food on his plate. "I don't know what all the rush is about," he continues. "You'd think there was a war on." He laughs at his own joke. He stuffs his paw with sausages and ham and walks over to the window to stare out through the bars. "It gives me the willies," he says.

"The war?"

"No, this fog. Can't see a thing out there."

I join him at the window. The market square outside is lost in the mist. "It's getting worse."

"I tell you, it just plain gives me the willies. I *hear* things, you know," he adds. "In the middle of the night."

"Please don't get him started," says Eli. I've never seen him look so pale.

Mr. McKenney stares out into the fog. "No telling what's out there," he says. "It could swallow you right up. I was in London once. Before we shipped over here, so must have been '75. The fog was so thick you couldn't see your hand in front of your face. Comrade of mine stepped out into it and never came back."

I speak in a soft voice so Eli doesn't have to hear. "He deserted?"

"No, he loved the army life. Just disappeared into the fog and was never seen again. And that night I heard the banshee."

"In London? You heard a banshee in London?"

"Thought I'd left them behind in Ireland." He shakes his head. "But city or country, there's nothing scarier than that voice wailing in the fog. It gives me the willies." He turns and looks around the room. "Where's that piss-pot?"

He unbuttons his trousers as he walks over to the corner. If I'm going to have time alone with Eli, now may be my only chance.

"Please can you do it outside, Mr. McKenney? The smell!"

Mr. McKenney looks past me. "You want me to go out in *that*?"

Eli looks up. "The outhouse ain't far."

"And Ginger's out there too," I offer. "She'll keep you company."

"That dog doesn't like me."

"She'll be happy to see anyone," I say. "Eli has hardly touched his sausages. Maybe you can give her one."

I expect a reaction from Eli, but he doesn't even look up as he offers his plate.

Mr. McKenney looks at me, then back at Eli. "I'll have to lock you up. You know the drill."

Step-THUMP. I'm not going to let that get to me this time. Not in the middle of the day — even a day where the fog is as thick as tannery sludge. And nor do I rush over to Eli this time. Mr. McKenney returns and locks us in. His wooden leg thumps down the hallway and descends the stairs.

Eli looks up and his eyes are wide. "They wanna *hang* me, Slim." And then the words spill out of him. "You gotta get me out of here. We gotta go ahead with your plan. Maybe you could knock out Old Pegleg with spirits, the way you done me. Jake?"

This is real. That's what he once said to me. *No bear traps. No duelling pistols. This is real.*

"Eli, maybe we should just wait."

"Easier to do it now — before the jail's built."

"No, I mean maybe we should go through with the trial."

"*What?*"

"We should let justice prevail."

"What's that mean?"

"Prove you're innocent."

"Jake, they wanna *hang* me. You know what that does? If you're lucky, it snaps your neck. If you ain't lucky, you strangle."

"They have to find you guilty first."

"Either way, your feet dance in the air, Jake. And you know what else? Mr. McKenney says if it's treason they don't just hang you. They pull out your guts and they cut you in pieces. And they chop off your head and put it on a pole."

He's holding my wrists, and I feel the spray of his words on my cheek. I look down at his hands, then meet his eyes. "Did you sign a paper when you took the oath?"

But he's looking over my shoulder at the door. "That don't seem right, but that's what he says they do. Even to a boy."

"Did you sign your name?"

And he stops and looks at me closely.

"Jake, what are you talking about?"

"When you gave your oath, did you sign a paper?"

"Don't see what that's got to do with hanging."

"The court will see it differently."

"That's just the point. We gotta get out of here. Jake? Jake, you ain't getting soft on this, are you?" Now I'm the one staring at the floor. "Escape was *your* idea," he continues. "And it was a good one."

I still can't look up at him. "I've given it more thought."

"You think too much."

Now finally I lift my eyes and meet the disbelief in his. "There's a system of justice, Eli. We have to trust in it."

"What's there to trust? That muckety-muck from York?"

"It's the King's justice."

"No it ain't. It's William Dunwoody's pa and that muckety-muck. What've they been filling your head with, Jake? Or is it them law books?"

"You're not being reasonable."

"Me! What about you? You change direction like a weather vane."

"Trust me on this."

"*Trust you*? Trust the King's justice? I tell you this, Jake Gibson, the only one I trust is myself. I thought I could trust *you*. But I can't, and as far as — "

He stops. We both hold our breath, listening to the *step-THUMP* of Mr. McKenney coming up the stairs and down the hallway.

"You in there?" he shouts. Then he starts a string of oaths, many of which I've never heard before. The key rattles in the lock. "If they've . . . If somehow . . . I'll have their guts for garters," he shouts.

The door swings open. He stares at us. "What's wrong with you boys?" he says. "Someone just die?"

The List

November 1812

From the distance, the hammers pound; nearby, a crow caws, but I can see nothing in this fog — not the Dunwoody house across the street, not even Government House behind me. I follow Ginger, my hands groping in the damp air.

I try not to think of ghosts or banshees, but I end up thinking about Eli, and that's even worse. Standing on the edge of a wagon, his hands tied behind his back. His eyes find mine in panic, then they stuff a sack over his head and over the hemp knot. A drum rolls, a whip cracks and the wheels lurch forward.

Ginger's tail wags.

"Sakes!"

"Mina?"

"Jacob Gibson, I thought you gave up on scaring a girl like that."

Her shape forms in the fog — a shawl clutched around her shoulders against the mist.

"Did you see him just now?" she asks.

"Yeah. He's in a bad way."

"My pa?"

"No. I mean Eli. What did *you* mean?"

"I *saw* Pa again. Out here. In the street."

How to reply to that? "Mina — "

"I saw him. I'm sure I did. When the sun came through a moment ago. I saw him." What's she talking about? There's been no sun. The fog has been getting worse! "From the upstairs window," she continues. "Standing right about here." She looks back over her shoulder as if he might be waiting behind her.

I take a deep breath. "Mina, I don't think your father's here."

"I dunno, Jake. I just get a feeling sometimes and then I think I see him." She stops peering through the grey and she looks at me steadily. "What happened to your face?"

"Ginger bit me."

"What?"

"When they arrested Eli. I had to stop her from attacking the soldiers and she bit me."

"You forgive her?"

"Does she forgive *me*? That's more the point."

"Jake, my little brother's in trouble." Now, apart from saying that she's seen Mr. McCabe in this fog, this is about the stupidest thing I've ever heard. Of course Eli's in trouble — he's charged with high treason. But she continues, "I heard them talking."

"Who?"

"The Master and Sheriff Mansbridge. They were talking about Eli's trial and I didn't like the sound of it."

"What did they say?"

"Just come with me."

She knows her way back through the fog. We reach the front door of the Dunwoody house and I follow her inside.

"Wait here," she says. I stand in the lobby, with no one but the portraits to keep me company. Other than Government House, this is the grandest home in Newark, with its parquet floors and crystal chandelier. The windows are so high, you'd never think that glass was expensive. But when I look out this big window now, all I see is a grey wall of fog.

Mina returns down the stairs and offers me two sheets of paper.

"Where'd you get these?"

"From the Master's room. His desk. While I was dusting."

"I have no business seeing this."

"Just look, will you? I think it has something to do with Eli."

"It's just a list of names."

"What names? Some of them crossed out and some circled. Why?" The names are written in an elegant hand. In the margins, notes are scribbled in smaller handwriting and different ink. "They were talking last night — Mr. Mansbridge and the Master. Talking about Eli and the trial. Then Mr. Mansbridge left and the Master went back to his room, and this morning there was this paper on his desk."

I know this list, these names. Mr. Willcocks, Father and I worked on a similar one last summer before the election. I study the notes in the margins. *JJW support . . . Sound . . . Could be bought . . . Knows the defendant* — that last note is written beside Father's name, which has been crossed out like so many of the others.

"Jake, what's going on?"

"This is a voters' list, Mina."

"All them names voted last summer?"

"Yes, and the names of Mr. Willcocks's supporters have been crossed out."

"Why?"

"The names that are circled . . . Mina, these are the people who were big supporters of Mr. Ecker."

"Henry's brother, the one what run against Mr. Willcocks?" she asks

Why are Mr. Dunwoody and Sheriff Mansbridge interested in old elections? I turn to the second page. More names from Lincoln County, but written in the upper corner are names of three people I don't know: *Thomas Scott, William Campbell, William*

Dummer Powell. The first and second names have been crossed out. The third one is circled. And beneath it is written, again in that refined hand, *Discuss with JBR.*

"These three," I read them to her, "who are they? Who's JBR?"

"I don't know."

"These men have never been to the house?"

"Not that I recollect."

"I've heard these names before," I say.

"Where?"

"I don't remember."

"It's a puzzlement. But I tell you, Jake, it's got something to do with Eli."

Should I show this to Father? What if he became angry that we had taken Magistrate Dunwoody's paper? I can't take a chance at upsetting him, but I need some advice. I know just the man to turn to.

"We've got to show this to Mr. Willcocks," I say.

She shakes her head quickly. "I got to get it back before the Master returns."

"I won't be long."

"Jake, I can't. They'll come home any minute."

I take another look and try to memorize the margin notes, then I turn to go.

"Jake?"

I pause on the porch. She waits by the open door. "What is it?"

"Thank you," she says and she kisses me on the cheek.

Ginger and I hurry down the road through the fog and I'm not thinking of lists of names, or Mr. Willcocks, or fog and things that might be out there. I'm thinking of Mina's lips. And then, because I haven't been thinking about it, I remember where I've seen those three names before. I run toward Mr. Willcocks's house.

* * *

This room seems so empty now. The ceiling used to be looped with string where we hung newly printed pages to dry, and the big printing press we called The Beast once stood in the middle of the floor. The Beast is gone and the room next door is empty — no table where we set the galleys; no type case with its thousands of letters. Last summer, everything was sold and carted off to a man who lives farther down the lake. Now the room is littered with piles of other people's newspapers and stacks of books.

"Campbell, Scott and Powell: those are the three justices of Upper Canada, right?" I fetch the kettle as it whistles on the stove. "They'll judge Eli's case. Right?"

"One of them will."

Mr. Willcocks clears papers from the chair and places them on a stack in the corner. I heat the teapot and spoon in leaves. Mrs. Lovelace always insists on fresh tea. Mr. Willcocks uses his leaves again. I think these ones have been used often.

"Why is William Dummer Powell circled?"

"He's the toughest of the three. A real hanging judge, Powell."

"A hanging judge?"

He picks up a cup from the wash basin and frowns at it. He wipes it with his shirt-tail, then picks out another that apparently does not need further cleaning, and plunks the two down on the table beside the teapot.

"Don't count on the mercy of his court. If Eli's found guilty, Justice Powell will make sure he hangs. Let me see that cheek of yours. Healing aright? Right as roosters. And you, girl?" He smiles at Ginger. Her tail thumps on the floor, but she lowers her head like a supplicant. "Did you learn your lesson?"

"She's been moping ever since," I say.

"Your father tells me she won't leave your side. You're a good girl." He pats her on the head and her tail thumps harder. He nods for me to fetch the milk. One sniff and I prefer to have my tea black.

We used to gather like this in the afternoons — Mr. Willcocks, who owned the newspaper and wrote the articles, Mr. Kelly, who set the type, and Mr. Stephenson, who printed the pages.

I enjoyed the leisure hours afterward — "having

the *craic*," Mr. Willcocks called it — but now I chafe at the delay. Mr. Willcocks takes his seat, but I stand with my hands on the back of the chair, practically lifting my feet off the floor.

"Who's JBR? And why would he be interested in the voters' list?"

"JBR is the new attorney general," he replies.

"Bev Robinson?"

"John Beverley Robinson, to be precise."

"He wants to see Eli hang?"

Mr. Willcocks nods at me to sit and he waits for me to calm down. The tea is so hot, it scalds my lips. Mr. Willcocks watches the mist rise from his cup. He holds his cup and saucer like a gentleman. Surely Mrs. Lovelace would approve. "More than that." He settles back. "He wants to show justice at work."

"But why are they interested in the voters' list?"

He raises his eyes to mine and I know the answer.

"It's for the jury, right? They choose the jury from the list of voters."

"Very good, Jacob."

"And they want jurors who will find Eli guilty."

"Go on," he says. He takes his first sip of tea. "What can you tell me about my supporters last spring? And those who supported Mr. Ecker?"

"People voted for you because they thought you would stand up for our rights."

"Yes?"

"And they voted for Mr. Ecker if they thought we had to do more to get ready for war."

"That's correct. So, how do you think they'd feel about Eli?"

"Well, they sure don't like Americans." And then I see what would happen if the jury was chosen from the people whose names were circled on the list. "That's not fair!"

"Indeed! And tampering with a jury is against the law as well." He thinks a moment and I take my first sip of tea. He gives me a sad smile. "A newspaper would come in handy about now. Know anyone who has one?"

"You said you weren't going to sell the *Colonial Guardian* and then you did." He gives me a disheartened shrug. I think he probably misses his newspaper too. "Maybe you could buy another one. I'd work for you. We could tell the story of Eli's trial and make sure it was fair."

His smile turns warmer. "Jacob, if it was up to you and me, the world would be a better place."

"So," I blurt, "we'll tell the whole world. Let's start another newspaper. Right now!"

"Jacob, I'd have to buy a printing press. The only place where I would get one is the United States. And under the current circumstances" — he pours more tea into his cup — "that's unlikely."

I rise to my feet, pacing the boards. My steps echo in the empty room.

"We have to tell someone. Tell Mr. Robinson." I look back at Mr. Willcocks. "Or is he behind all of this?"

Mr. Willcocks puckers his lips as if he's just eaten something sour. "That prim little martinet? He'll want everything fair and square. More likely it's Magistrate Dunwoody and his friends, working behind Robinson's back."

"Then we'll tell Bev. He'll make it stop!"

Mr. Willcocks leans forward with his elbows on the table and chews on his lip as he considers. "I'd be more inclined," he says softly, "to take matters into our own hands."

* * *

The hammers have stopped pounding and the town is silent. The fog has lifted, but the sky grows darker. Lights shine at Government House and at Dunwoodys'.

"Ginger. This way." She tilts her head to look at me. She wants to go home, but first we need to make one last stop. No light in Eli's room. Mr. McKenney won't be there, playing chess. Loon call, then three hoots from an owl. The window opens behind the iron bars.

"That you out there, Jake Gibson?"

"Down here. By the bushes."

"Leave me alone."

"We're going to get you out, Eli."

"Go away or I'll call the guard."

"We've got to work together on this."

"I can't trust you. You keep changing your mind."

"Trust me on this. I promise." I can see him only as a dark shape in the darkness upstairs. He doesn't move for some time and I think: *Am I going to be able to keep this promise?* Father made me promise to stay with the Lovelace family when he went off to the battle, but I sneaked away with him. I made a promise that I would go back to Mohawk Village with Good Spirit's remains. It's a promise that I could not keep. I made a promise in the church that I would obey Father and follow his example, but now, if we go ahead with this, I'll break that promise too. Maybe Eli's right. Why should he trust my promises?

Then he says, "I know a man with a wooden leg named McKenney."

* * *

I lie awake and look out the window at a sliver of moon and bright stars. Father must never know what I'm about to do. Mr. Willcocks will know, but he's not going to tell anyone. I'll have to tell Mina too. If Eli escapes, the fingers will point to her. Maybe she'll have some kind of a plan — heaven knows we could use one.

My eyes are heavy and I feel myself floating. Merciful sleep. Sleep that heals from the inside out and from the bottom to the top. And it feels like it's a dreamless sleep and maybe I'll get through the night without being haunted.

Then I'm there again: the forest, the smoke, the gunfire and war cries. It's not smoke; it's fog, growing thicker and darker. I can't see as far as the next tree and the noises fade away, except for one long, high wail — growing louder, closer. A dark shape moves toward me, wailing and crying. The banshee has arrived. And there in the grass, a crow looks up at me with intelligent eyes. Mountain Lion leans over the shattered body of Good Spirit. He closes the boy's eyes, then folds his hands over his chest.

I kneel beside Ronhnhí:io. His face is sculpted in candle wax. His hands are the shore stones on a winter morning. Mountain Lion motions me to stop, but I reach out and gently touch the wound where the blood oozes from his breast. I bring my fingers to my lips. Taste. Salt.

Ronhnhí:io opens his eyes and he looks at me. A sheltered fire in a November rain. Every muscle in his body is still as death.

I want to flee, but I cannot move. It is as if I am a salamander whose blood is too cold, while all around me the hot-blooded spirits look on. I am vulnerable, their prey, and there's nothing I can do to protect myself.

But he smiles at me. His lips do not move but I hear his words clear in my head: You are afraid. Everyone is afraid. That is your weapon. You are a warrior now.

Wedding

December 1812

General Brock used to sit on this rock, staring out into this dark water. Eli and I would hide in those bushes and wonder what he was thinking about. Downstream, the bulrushes spike from the frozen shallows. Everyone is sleeping — everyone but me.

Good Spirit, can you hear me now? Or are you drifting down this great river on your voyage into the night? We all must travel that voyage. The warriors who attacked the villages on these shorelines in the days of flint arrows, they have gone into the night. The explorers, armed with the iron crucifix, following the sound of the big water, they have gone into the night. The traders portaging the Falls with their trinkets and mirrors, the armies of white coats and gold lilies who built the castle at the river mouth. Gone. Into the night. The redcoat armies and greencoat refugees who cleared the land and built a town, they have not all gone, but they weaken with age and will take that voyage soon.

And these I have seen with my own eyes. General Brock and Colonel Macdonell, sabres flashing briefly in the sun, they have gone into the night. The men in the bateau drifting in black water. The terrified soldiers who fled to the edge of the cliffs with the shrieking warriors in pursuit.

I once felt the pull of the river when I fell through the ice on a winter day, so long ago. But I stared through frozen eyelashes at the face of the boy who would not let me go into that night. Eli, I owe you my life and I cannot let them take you. I promise. Good Spirit, are you listening?

I cut this hand and drop this blood into the river, and the blood disappears into the night.

* * *

"A little less talking and a lot more digging," Mr. McKenney calls over the pounding of hammers.

Now that the walls of the new courthouse and jail are up, the construction has moved indoors, but Eli and I work out here in the wind. Mr. McKenney stays huddled near his campfire.

Eli straightens up and gives a little wave, then bends forward to thrust the shovel into the earth again. "Corn, Slim," he resumes in a low voice, "ain't no way that'll work."

"It's all I have right now." I blow on my fingers to keep them warm, then take my shovel again.

"We gotta think of something else." Eli heaves another shovelful. Pebbles splatter on the ground. "Maybe just dig this here hole into a tunnel. Take it all the way to the jailhouse."

"Tunnel from the jailhouse to the outhouse? You'd wind up in the bottom of all that . . . that . . . "

"Won't nobody go snooping around that end of it."

"How would you hide the other entrance?" I ask.

"A trap door in the jailhouse floor."

"I guess we'd better get jobs on the inside crew."

"Reckon we gotta dig this hole first."

"All right, you two, if you're talking, I want to hear what you're saying." Mr. McKenney hobbles over and stands on the mound Eli and I have piled outside the hole.

"Ain't nothing special, Mr. McKenney." Eli raises his voice over the pounding of hammers. "Jake's telling me about the wedding. Did you know he's gonna have two sisters?"

"You just never mind that, and you finish this hole. I won't be waiting here with you all morning." He stares up at the gloomy sky. "Looks like rain."

"Or snow," I offer. "Better finish this before the ground freezes, Eli."

Mr. McKenney grunts and looks longingly at the courthouse, where the carpenters work in the warmth. "You two just keep digging," he says as he heads back toward his fire. "Remember: keep it deep and square."

I lean on the shovel. "Eli, we've got to try my plan, at least."

It's not much of a plan. Mr. McKenney has a vivid imagination when it comes to ghosts and goblins, banshees and bogies. I think we can spook him long enough for me to slip into Government House and get the key. I could hide with it until . . .

Yeah. Eli's right. It's pretty far-fetched.

Eli tries to smile. "We'll try, Slim. You just tell me what I got to do."

"The important part is to get into the attic when you hear my signal. If we work together, we can do it."

"Reckon," he says without enthusiasm.

"Do you think you could smuggle something up there?"

"What?"

"Something big as a cannonball?"

"A small one, maybe."

"Doesn't have to be big."

"So, when you get me out, how we gonna cross the river?"

"I'm working on that."

"You gonna row me yourself?" He looks doubtful.

"I said I'm working on it."

"So what are you working on?"

"I can't tell you."

He narrows his eyes. "You got someone else with you on this?"

"I can't tell you, Eli."

He turns back to the work. His face is red. There's lots of things I haven't been able to tell him. It all started with the secret mission to Mohawk Village.

"You just say what to do, Jake," he mutters to the dirt. Then, "Hey, what's that?" He kneels down and picks something out of the bottom of the hole.

"Let me see." A flint arrowhead rests on the palm of my hand.

"How long you think it's been there, Slim?"

"Flint? That deep? Hundreds of years. Maybe even more than that."

"Reckon?"

"I could show it to Dominie Burns. He might know."

Eli takes the arrowhead from my palm and studies it.

"Naw." He reaches into his shirt and pulls out the pouch I gave him.

"You still have it?"

He shrugs and puts the arrowhead inside the pouch.

"Who's that?" he asks.

I turn. Ginger runs up to us with her tongue lolling and a big grin on her doggie face. And behind her . . .

"Just Abby," I say.

"*She's* gonna be your stepsister? You never told me she was pretty."

Abby, pretty? I always thought that George was the pretty one.

In her arms she carries a wicker basket covered with a checkered cloth. Mr. McKenney rises from the campfire and intercepts her, but she gives him a warm smile and offers him something from the basket — I can't see what it is. As they continue toward us, Eli climbs out of the hole.

"Here, Jacob. I brought you some lunch."

"For Mr. McKenney too?"

"Why would we not?" She gives Mr. McKenney another smile, then glances at Eli and looks quickly away. Is she blushing?

"I thank you kindly, Miss Lovelace," says the old soldier. "I'll leave you young people to have your lunch in peace." Abby and I watch him until he returns to his campfire, but Eli is watching me.

"Ain't you gonna introduce us?"

"Abby, this is Eli McCabe."

"The notorious traitor." She *is* blushing. "Mama says I'm not to speak to you."

"Miss Abby ain't talking to me, Slim. She's talking to you."

Abby tries to stifle a smile. "Do you think Master McCabe would like some lunch?"

"Jake," he says, "did I mention I'm getting real hungry?"

We take shelter behind the boards of the courthouse, while the jailer looks on from the campfire.

"Does your friend like sausage? Cheese?" She breaks away pieces of bread.

"Jake, I'm quite partial to sausage, but I gotta say I do love cheese." He reaches into the basket and pulls out a stoneware jug. He warms his hands around it.

"Hot milk?" she asks.

She fills a pottery mug and we pass it around. Eli has a white moustache.

"Will the jail be finished before the wedding?" asks Abby.

"They're working fast — but not that fast."

"It's a race," says Eli. "Who's going to be imprisoned first: me or Jake's pa?"

I snicker. "You're the one who said Father would remarry."

"That's a fact. Women's a civilating influence."

Eli glances over at Abby. Her frown cows him.

"We shall move in with Jacob before Christmas. That makes sense, I suppose. I just find the haste so unseemly." I don't know what to say to that. Neither does Eli, but he stares as if each word shines like sunlight dappled on the lake. "And Mama wants to make such a big event of it," Abby continues. "A ball, no less."

"I don't like dancing," I grumble.

"I *love* to dance," says Eli. "You think they'd let me come?"

"The grass hasn't grown on Papa's grave and Mama wants to invite all society."

"You should have a shivaree," Eli says.

"What's that?" she replies. Then she raises her hand to her mouth and turns to face me. "What's that, Jacob?"

"Everyone dresses up," says Eli. "Makes lots of noise."

"Oh," says Abby, "a charivari."

"Making lots of noise?" he asks.

"Yeah," I reply. "Outside the bedroom."

"Same thing then. You folks talk funny."

"My room will be next door," says Abby. "How am I going to sleep?"

"I reckon you'd be a shivaree-er, Miss Abby, not a shivaree-ee. Eeee. Ee."

And Abby laughs. It occurs to me that I've never heard her laugh before. She turns to me. "Your friend has an unusual way with words." She collects the mug, the jug and the napkins and places them carefully back in the basket. "Master McCabe, it was a pleasure meeting you — even if we did not speak to each other."

She offers her hand. Eli hesitates. He takes her fingers and raises them to his lips. And she laughs again, like the trickle of water in the spring.

We watch her walk away and Eli says, "Corn, Slim, I'd slay dragons for her."

* * *

"If anyone can show just cause," intones the Reverend Mr. Addison, "why this couple cannot lawfully be joined together in matrimony" — he pauses and gazes around the room for effect — "let him speak now or forever hold his peace."

Silence. What would happen if someone did step forward? *Stop the wedding!*

But who would do it? George beams her approval. Mrs. Dunwoody stands beside Mrs. Lovelace like a plump matron. She will sign the witness papers with the satisfaction of a merchant who knows a good deal when she sees one. Mr. Willcocks stands on the other side of Father and he steals a glance at me and winks. None of them will break the peace. Nor will Abby, even though she thinks the wedding is happening too soon. And I won't either. You have to hold your peace even if you don't want another family moving into your house.

I've studied the law. You can speak now if you can prove that either Father or Mrs. Lovelace is still legally married to someone else. Who can prove that?

Still, that *would* be something! The church door flies open, and the ghost of Mr. Lovelace stands there in the aisle in his winding sheet, the grave dirt covering his clothes and the flesh rotting from his bones. He staggers up the aisle, slime trailing behind him. At the altar, he seizes his lawfully wedded wife and carries her away to the realms of the dead.

What's happening here? I'm thinking these terrible thoughts, but I am not afraid. In fact, I'm playing with my imagination. And as this thought crosses my mind, I get a feeling someone is watching me. I turn in the pew. No one is there, but in my head, a voice says, *You are afraid. That is your weapon now.* And another voice says, *Take care of my boy.*

Mr. Addison's voice rings in the rafters, "I now pronounce you Man and Wife."

* * *

So it's done. They're now Mr. and Mrs. Robert Gibson, and I have a stepmother and stepsisters. The wedding this morning was a quiet affair, but this ball shows the world how far we have all come. The men and women smile at one another as they go through the steps, skipping and laughing. George and Abby are having a wonderful time. George is too young to have a dance card of her own, but that doesn't stop the young men from inviting her to join them for a cotillion. I slouch at the side table. Even at the best of times, I don't like to dance, and this is certainly not the best of times.

"When do we leave?" Mina asks.

"Any time now. You enjoying yourself?"

"I'm too nervous."

"Me too."

Father and my stepmother have left for home, and soon the mummers will gather with their masks and their pots and pans. How many will join the charivari tonight? All day the weather has grown worse as the wind shifts from the north. With enough rum punch and homebrew, a crowd will gather on Prideaux Street nonetheless.

William Dunwoody picks his way over, a little unsteady on his feet.

"Good evening, Miss Mina." He bows. She rises and curtsies — something I haven't seen her do before.

"How do you do, Young Master?"

"Oh, please." He smiles. "Let's dispense with the formalities tonight."

"Yes, sir."

"You used to call me *William*. Please, do so again."

"Yes, William."

"Goodness, you make it sound so formal. Gibson, I hope you won't mind if Miss Mina joins me for a dance."

Not now, I think. *We've got to get out of here.*

"I'd be delighted," she says and she nods to me as she takes his hand and leaves with him for the dance line. She may not be dressed as well as the other women, but she dances more gracefully than anyone. Where did she learn the steps? She's been watching how things are done in that house. But she's still on the floor and now it's time. Amid all the dancing, no one sees me slip out the door.

Charivari

December 1812

The winds have dropped and the chill remains in the air as the first flakes of winter float down from a dark sky. Didn't Mina understand the plan? It didn't include dancing with William Dunwoody! Will Henry take a turn as well?

Behind me, the shrill of whistles and wail of the fiddles move from tune to tune. William Dunwoody is getting value from this dance. Ahead, laughter, the clang of spoons upon pots, and the barking of one very annoyed dog, carry in the darkness. It's begun: the dockers and towners will all be out tonight in full charivari, dressed up in their costumes and parading around our house. How many people are out there? That part of the plan is going as expected.

I turn from the road into the burying grounds. Snowflakes fall on my eyelashes as the ground turns white. I come to a grave — cold marble in the snow and decayed leaves. Mother and Charlotte are buried here, and William, Mary Ellen and Elizabeth, who all died when I was very young. The sheets are tucked by the stone where I hid them. I slip mine over my head and it adds a layer of warmth.

Wish we had arranged to meet somewhere else. But I will not be afraid. Fear is *my* weapon now. Still, I wish I didn't have to wait here.

"Ready?"

I yelp, startled. At least Mina has left the dance.

"Ha!" she says. "'Bout time I got you back for all the times you've scared me."

"You took your time saying your goodbyes."

"Yup. Poor William. He has no idea. Wanted to meet me afterward."

"What did you say?"

"Told him to watch for my candle. He's in for a long night."

I hand her a sheet and she lifts it over her head and pulls it down. Through the eyeholes, she winks, and I turn toward town. We're leaving tracks. I hadn't counted on those. But the snow is coming faster now. Our trail will be covered soon.

* * *

The clanging and banging and laughter grow louder, but at the corner of King Street, we turn away from the revelry and up toward Queen Street.

"Stop stepping on me."

"Sakes, Jake. How'm I s'posed to see where I'm going?"

I lift the sheet from my face. Mina does the same. The snow comes more fiercely and the noise from the mummers falters. *Don't stop. Not yet!* The storm hides the Dunwoody residence, but lights glow in two windows of Government House — one on the main floor and one upstairs.

"Jake, I got to tell you, this has got to be the dumbest idea ever."

"Shh."

I give a loon call, then three owl hoots. Stupid loon to be up north this time of year. Stupid owl to be out in this storm. But a silhouette appears upstairs, raises its right hand to wave, then slips back out of the frame, and the light goes out.

You are afraid. Everyone is afraid. That is your weapon. You are a warrior now.

"You aright, Jake?" says Mina.

I nod my head but don't trust my voice to speak — just gesture with my chin toward the market square — and we part. I flatten myself against the wall below the downstairs window. The stone feels cold even through my sheet and overcoat.

Through slanting swaths of falling snow, Mina walks toward the market square. She moves like she could tiptoe on lily pads. If I ever wanted to dance, I would dance with her. The cotton sheet trails over the powder as she moves her arms slowly up and down, and a soaring osprey is not so graceful. But her shoes leave footprints in the snow.

It's time. From below the sill, I issue a low, pain-filled moan. It starts in my belly and it rises to my chest as I raise the pitch, then lower it again. "WhoooaaAAAoohh."

No reaction. Has Mr. McKenney heard it inside? I begin again, louder this time, and the final note ends at a higher pitch.

"WhoooooaaAAAAAOOHHH."

The light on the first floor shifts and brightens. Curtains open wide and the candlelight shines across the snow. I press myself against the wall.

"You see anything?" says a voice inside.

Is Mr. McKenney there? If so, he's not alone tonight. This could turn out badly. But I remember how we stoked each other's fear on All Hallows' Eve: the plan might work even better.

Mr. McKenney's voice replies, "There's something out there. In the market square."

"What is it?"

"I can't tell you. Not with all the snow."

"Didn't sound like it was coming from the market square," says a third voice.

"That's a fact," Mr. McKenney replies. "It gives me the willies, all the same."

"None of your fairy stories, McKenney," says the

third voice. "It's my deal. Spades are trump."

"Probably Gibson's wedding," says Mr. McKenney. "There's a charivari tonight."

"Play."

"Yes, I'm sure that's what it is." The light dims from the window. "A charivari."

I find a new hiding spot in the lilac bushes. Off in the market square, Mina dances closer to the building, but I can barely see her through the white.

This time I start with a shriek — much louder than before — and end with a moan.

"WHHAAAAAOOooohhhhh."

The lantern returns to the window, and this time the sash lifts and a head pokes out into the snowstorm.

"Who's out there? Identify yourself!"

The only reply comes from upstairs — at the top of the building. A *thump* as loud as a cannonball hitting an attic beam.

"What's that?"

"Best go upstairs and see to young McCabe."

It thumps again, this time halfway to the other side of the building.

I give the same low moan, this time in a deeper voice.

"WHHAAAAAOOooohhhhh."

Across the market square, Mina sings a high note, as mad as Shakespeare's Ophelia.

"Laaaaaa . . . La la la."

"Jeeze, McKenney, what's out there?"

"You check outside. I'll go upstairs."

"I'm not going out there."

The sound of the cannonball thumps in the far corner.

"What's going on up there?"

"Ah, he's just having us on."

"But what's that *outside*?"

"Mummers, McKenney. Just mummers. You're not scared by some children having a fright night?"

"Well then, you come look. It's like nothing I've ever seen."

"Jaysus!"

I can hardly see through the snow now, but my heart races. Is Mina out there alone? She dances as if she's with someone else. The snow is too thick to see. From the upper floor of the building comes a sound like I've never heard — a cry of despair and fear, starting high and falling, fading.

"AAAAAHIIIEeeeeeeee."

A cry that contains all the sorrow of a life lost and loved ones never to be seen. And it's suddenly cut short by the *thud* of a cannonball dropped onto wood. Quick now.

I scramble to my knees and dash around the corner. The snow stings my eyes and I pull the sheet over my head and adjust it to find the eyeholes. The front door is not locked but it's heavy. The wind catches it and it swings before me.

"AAAARRRRHHHHHhhhhhhh . . . "

The cry of someone falling is repeating now. And from the top of the stairs comes a *thump.* Is it the sound of Mr. McKenney's wooden leg on the wooden floor? Could he possibly be up there? I hadn't counted on that. I hitch up the sheet to keep from tripping as I sprint up the stairs two at a time.

The ring of keys hangs on a peg above the table at the top of the stairs. I grab it and hurry for the door at the end of the hall. The pounding continues. Eli had better be ready to move, whatever he's doing in there to make these sounds.

The first key does not fit. The second one does. The door swings open and he's there, fully dressed and ready. Run! I lead the way down the hallway. The door slams behind us.

Will Mr. McKenney and the others confront us? But the door to the guardroom is shut tight. They've closed it to barricade themselves against whatever they fear is making the noise.

We sprint into the street.

The Lighthouse

December 1812

Snow caps the tombstones and shrouds the dead grass in the burying grounds. A white figure runs toward us through the darkness, black hair catching the driving snow. Mina and Eli hug, then I pass him a sheet and he pulls it over his head. We're three charivari ghosts now, peeking through our eyeholes, hurrying down the road toward the Navy Yard.

"Listen!" says Mina and she raises her hand. We stop.

"I don't hear nothing," says Eli.

"That's right," I say. No more music coming from Fort George. The dancing is over. But the wind now carries another sound — voices and laughter coming down the road toward us.

"Boney was a General,
Away hey ya,
A randy dandy general,
Jean François!"

Eli and Mina hesitate. We could hide by the side

of the road, and the white sheets would help us blend with the snow. But Mr. McKenney and the others will be on our trail by now. So I step forward. William Dunwoody, Henry Ecker and John Beverley Robinson stagger arm in arm in arm, singing their hearts out.

"Boney fought the Roos-i-ans,
Away hey ya,
The Austrians and Proos-i— "

"Hello!" says the attorney general of Upper Canada. "What's this?"

The three stumble to a halt and support one another upright while they gaze at us. Henry carries a lantern and he totters forward unsteadily as he shines it on us. I step forward. I wave my arms up and down and caper a few dance steps. Eli and Mina cavort behind me.

"The charivari," says William.

"How quaint," says Mr. Robinson. "Splendid. Simply splendid. Hello, ghosties!"

"You folks looking for the Gibson place?" adds Henry. "You're going in the wrong direction. Prideaux Street. Down the road past the new courthouse."

I nod my assent, but I don't stop dancing.

"I think one of them's a girl," says William. "Good evening, Miss. Care to join us? We can protect you from these ghosties."

"And the cold." Henry smirks.

"Gentlemen," interrupts Mr. Robinson, "I believe

Mr. Dunwoody already has an assignation."

William's head jerks back in indignation. "Who told you that?"

"Relax, my friend. No one tells me these things. I simply observe."

"Rude to keep a lady waiting," adds Henry.

"Goodnight, ghosties." John Beverley Robinson tips his top hat and breaks into song as they weave their way toward town. Soon the others join in.

"Boney was a Corsican,
Away hey ya,
A roaring snorting Corsican,
Jean François!"

As we sprint down the road to the Navy Yard, my shoes slip in the snow, but I don't lose my footing. On the dock waits a man, huddled against the wind. He rises to his feet and untethers a rowboat.

* * *

I can no longer see the shoreline. We're alone in the mutinous water with snow slashing against our faces. Mr. Willcocks's shoulders heave as he rows. The snow sticks to his hands where he grips the oars, and the sleet grows thicker on his coat. In the stern, Eli strips away his sheet and for a moment his clothes stand out black against the snow. He shivers and cuddles up against Mina. She wraps the sheet over his back.

I turn and look forward. Somewhere out there is a riverbank. The water carries patches of slush that rest on the surface for a moment, then sink into the black. The current pushes us from the right, and Mr. Willcocks guides the bow upstream to compensate. But who knows where we will land?

The oarlocks squeak in complaint against Mr. Willcocks's powerful strokes. I can see nothing to measure our progress — only the endless white snow and the swift black water. And then, swooping out of the darkness, something pokes me in the face and I tumble into the gunwale. We grind to a halt amid the scraping and groaning of wood on wood.

"We're here," says Mr. Willcocks in a harsh whisper. "Try downstream. I think."

I spring to my feet and grip the cold wood as I leap over the side. I crash through branches and sticks and hit the water with a gasp. It's freezing! But shallow — only to my knees — though the current wants to pull me deeper. Eli splashes down beside me and yelps. We each grab the bow rope as the boat draws us downstream. Are we going to lose it? But another splash and another pair of hands as Mina joins us to hold tight and shove our way through the branches.

Twenty yards and we find a beach and haul the rope while Mr. Willcocks heaves at the oars. The keel scrapes on pebbles. He stows the oars, leaps out beside us and all four pull as the boat grudgingly leaves the current.

"The road is above that rise," says Mr. Willcocks. Our heads huddle close together. "Their sentry post is about two hundred yards to the left. Stay low to the ground, shout loud and keep shouting. You don't want them to shoot you in the dark."

Eli nods. Mina looks at me.

"Yes," I tell her. "I'm coming that far."

"It's safer if you go back now," she says.

"I'm coming with you. That far."

"Thanks, Jake." She leans forward and kisses me, this time on the lips. In the cold and sleet, her lips are soft and warm and for a moment I forget that my pant legs are freezing and the sleet is melting down my neck.

Eli jabs me in the ribs. "Ain't no time to waste."

Mr. Willcocks stays with the boat while the three of us crunch over the gravel and the snow, slipping our way uphill. The sleet falls less fiercely now and the wind is dropping. The line of trees at the top of the rise must be the road. I turn, and in the distance, a small light pulses so briefly that I wonder if my mind is playing tricks. But I watch and wait, and so do Eli and Mina. It flashes again.

"The lighthouse?" asks Mina.

Eli says, "Welcome to America." We watch in silence until the light pulses again — clearer this time; the storm is ending. "You could come with me, you know."

I shake my head. "Father's going to need me."

"Reckon." After a pause he says, "You think they'll know it was you?"

"They'll blame me," says Mina. She looks at the two of us. "I'll wait up top, little brother."

"Keep your head down," I remind her.

When she's out of earshot, Eli draws me close and puts his arm over my shoulder. "Didn't think you could pull it off, Slim, but you did."

"We all did. How did you make those sounds?"

"I thought the cannonball was gonna crash right through the ceiling."

"Who did the screaming?"

"Slim, you'd scream too — in the dark with all them spiders."

I turn my head and peer through the darkness, and I think I see Mina up the slope, walking toward the fort. Is someone walking beside her?

"Thanks, Slim. For saving my life, I mean."

"You'd do the same for me."

"That's a fact."

And then, from the darkness, a voice rings out.

"Who goes there? Identify yourself!"

Eli and I drop to the ground.

"Friend!" Mina calls from the roadway. "Help me, sir. Please!"

"Identify yourself," repeats the voice.

"Wilhelmina McCabe. My pa's with the New York militia."

"Step forward. I want to see your hands above your head."

"Don't shoot me, sir. I reckon I done had the scare of my life already tonight."

Eli and I stay flat on the ground.

"She'll have them come back for me when it's safe," he says.

"I've got to go."

"Reckon." He rises to his hands and knees, then sits upright. "One thing: I got something for you."

He reaches into his shirt and passes the small bag to me.

"You're gonna need it more than me," he says.

"I'll be aright."

"Right as roosters." He grins.

I feel the once-familiar shape and squeeze it the way I used to do. It has a different feel to it.

Then a voice calls out from the darkness up the road. "Eli McCabe? Identify yourself and step forward."

"It's safe, little brother. We're home now."

What do we do now? Shake hands? He clasps mine in his, but we draw each other forward and our arms are around each other's backs. Then he straightens up, turns and walks away from me into the darkness.

After a few steps he turns back and waves. "I'll be back," he calls.

"You've said that before."

"Kept my word, didn't I?"

"Always."

I try to see through the night and follow their voices as they move away toward the American fort. The snow has stopped. A full moon peeks through the clouds, and for a moment, the whole world seems white and pure. Then the clouds cover the moon again.

So this is the United States of America. It doesn't look different from our side of the river. I could follow this road south to places I never expected to see. Somewhere at the end of this road is Buffalo, where the McCabes have made their new home. And out there somewhere are the big cities on the seaboard, and the steamboats churning up the Hudson, and the mountains of Kentucky. The mills on the Susquehanna where they make the long rifles, and the legislature on the Potomac where they order the armies to fight us. Somewhere out there are the cotton plantations and the slave gangs and the Mississippi River that flows south toward summer. It's a direction that I had never thought to explore until now.

Eli and Mina are on their way into that other world. I watch them until they turn a corner in the road and disappear behind the trees. When I'm sure they have gone, I plow through the snow back down to the boat.

"There you are, young Gibson. I was beginning to wonder whether you were coming back."

"Thanks, Mr. Willcocks. Thanks for helping them."

"It was the least I could do."

We push the boat back into the water and I sit in the stern this time. My fingers toy with the pouch Eli gave me. I open it and feel inside. My finger scrapes along a sharp edge of the arrowhead from that hole Eli and I dug.

I study Mr. Willcocks's face as he strains at the oars. If he is worried about being caught, he sure doesn't show it. Calm as a lion. Then I look past him toward the pulse of the lighthouse.

Author's Note

The imagination works in funny ways. It grows from seeds of historical fact — a lighthouse once stood at Mississauga Point; the bombardment of Newark burned down the courthouse; General Brock sent Joe Willcocks to negotiate with the community at Mohawk Village. Many gifted historians have planted those seeds in my imagination, including the late Robert Malcomson, with his study of the Battle of Queenston Heights, and Carl Benn, with his work on the Iroquois and the War of 1812.

Many of the flowers don't look quite like the pictures from the historians' seed catalogues. John Beverley Robinson did not prosecute traitors following Queenston Heights — the treason trials would come later. Joe Willcocks did not send someone to Mohawk Village, but conducted his negotiations from his sickbed in a tavern. And certainly no one disturbed the solemnity of General Brock's funeral!

My special thanks to Paula Whitlow and Tara Froman of the Woodland Cultural Centre in Brantford for their wisdom and advice, and to Margaret Cook-Peters for providing the meaning and the pronunciation for the name Ronhnhí:io.

I have used the current term *Haudenosaunee* for the Six Nations, which Euroamericans referred to as the Iroquois. At the time, the Six Nations referred to themselves as Onkwehonwe.

Finally, thanks to my kid-crit groups both online and in Ottawa (you'll be hearing their names as their books emerge), to the soldiers and sweethearts of the Canadian Volunteers, to Paula McCann, Ciara Hall, Mercedes Ballem, Karen Hill and Iain Mitchell, to Sally Harding of the Cooke Agency and Sandy Bogart Johnston of Scholastic Canada, and to the readers of Jake and Eli's first book, *Brothers at War*, who have written to me in their eagerness to find out what happens next.

Finalist, Geoffrey Bilson Award
for Historical Fiction